Orgasm!

The Female Erotika Reader:
Hot Sex Stories to Make Her Steam

by Scarlet Blue

EB

Erotika Books
Los Angeles, CA

Copyright 2011 – Scarlet Blue

Library of Congress Cataloging-in-Publication Data

Orgasm! The Female Erotika Reader: Hot Sex Stories to Make Her Steam by Scarlet Blue

ISBN: 978-1-936828-19-7 (Softcover)

First Edition March 2011

A Romantic Evening

He was was sitting across from her but pretending to read the morning paper. He'd look at her while she did her daily paperwork noticing how beautiful her features still were. She still had her long hair, but not that long and it was not only her face that caught his attention.

Those eyes, the pretty blue ones he fell in love with years before which drew his attention to her once again. She continued on as he pretended to read as she wrote. He studied her lips and her facial structure which never seemed to change. He told himself it been a while since the two of them really laid down and snuggled. He told himself it had been a while since the two of them undressed and cuddled even. He knew she still loved him dearly.

He knew her body was in great shape. He'd seen her naked a number of times. He knew she was still trim after 16 years of marriage and that she hadn't lost it in any way. Her curves, her breasts, her long winding hips, and her thighs were as gorgeous today as they'd been years before and this is why they had the two children. He smiled and felt like telling her his thoughts. He folded the paper and put it down. She continued to work.

"You're still gorgeous you know" he said. She'd heard him as she continued to work. "Want to go to the bedroom…and make love?"

She put down her pen slowly raising her head to look at her husband. "Is that your best come on?" she asked smiling. He smiled and winked a wink she always loved. Still in a blouse and skirt, she put down her pen and stood. "Okay, I guess" she told him as if she was offering herself up but only as a chore as his wife. "I suppose I could."

He knew better and once she came around the desk, once she reached his side he took her hand lightly. She waited. He led her to their bedroom. Before sliding into bed, he turned her around. She was smiling again. Waiting for his best move he figured. He undid the top button of her blouse. She watched his eyes and his face, still smiling and trying to take in the moments. She closed them and took in a deep breath of air. She exhaled. She dearly loved her husband. He was kind and caring and he did almost everything he could to be there when he could. Today he was there for the family although the family wasn't home. It was only her and him. The two kids were with friends for the night.

"You have no idea how crazy I am about you still do you?" he said.

Quietly she said back to him "I think I do" but smiled again as she said it.

He kissed her lips softly but for a long while. She loved those soft kisses and kissed him back almost the same way. "How are your partners?" he said out of no where trying to be congenial as his foreplay skills deteriorated. She told him to not worry about them, to simply undress her. She told him to simply get her undressed. All she wanted was him against her. All she wanted was his body, his love, and all the fascinating sex they used to have all the time once again.

Could he do that, he asked himself. God those days were amazing. How they could seem to go on for hours at a time and he could sustain himself while she obtained orgasm after orgasm and then BAM, he finally came inside her. That part was the most terrific part of it all. Feeling him explode in her life he would...that was the most terrific portion of it of it all. She smiled.

He started to tell her something as he undid her fourth button. She put a finger to his lips. "All I want is you, your body, and us naked and wildly shuffling across one another while I feel this" and she put the palm of her hand down across his soft crotch. "All I want is you and your undying love and this... That's what I want honey."

Both smiled and he winked at her. He undid her last two buttons and saw her beautiful upper body. So trim, so full, and still so curvy in all its special ways...he could feel himself wanting her more and more. What was she thinking and feeling, he wondered? "What are you feeling right now?" he said.

Her eyes glassed over and a gentle smile crossed her face. She told him she wanted to lie down against him and play around. He liked that idea. Her nakedness against his... What a nice way to spend and evening with someone you truly love and admire. He pulled her in.

5

Holding her closely and lovingly, he kissed her lips and she kissed him back hard too, her hands floating in his hair as if she never felt it before. He undid his shirt and pulled it off. He pulled off his t-shirt and she looked at the sleek bare chest.

"Mmmmm, still a man in my book" she told him.

"Good" he replied. "I would hope so."

"Don't worry...there aren't any others out there that measure up to you."

With her shirt undone and her bra still on, his hand flirted upwards on her stomach. She felt it and her eyes slowly closed as she felt it coming closer to her breasts. Touch them, squeeze them she thought. Uhhh ohhhhhhh god yes... Feel my boobs honey...touch them, she told herself. They took hold of her bra covered boobs lightly massaging them back and forth and up and down. "Mmmmmm" she said softly. "I like how you do that to me."

They gazed at each other as her hands dropped to undo his belt. She undid his pants and they fell to the ground. He stepped out of them as his hands lovingly patted across her boobs and upper body. He then undid her skirt and it fell down to the ground too. "Ready?" she asked. He smiled and told her always. They laughed quietly and slipped in to the bed. He pulled her body close and before she knew it he was kissing her madly. "Mmmmmm I always have loved how you kiss me" she said.

"Me too... I mean how we kiss that is" he said back to her and continued to kiss her.

Before he knew it, her bra was undone and found its way to the bed. Her beautiful swelling breasts unfolded before him and he found himself crossing over them with his mouth. He loved her more then ever and she loved him as much. She loved pining his chest as she kissed it and rubbed it fondly.

On top of him she leaned down on him to kiss his stomach. He lay feeling her tender kisses but watching her breasts as they hung waiting

6

for him to take control of them. He always and still does, love them, and he grabbed hold of them while she kissed and petted his upper body.

"You still enjoy this?" she asked. He said nothing. "Well do you?" He still did nothing. "Oh come one…stop that" she told him. She noticed his eyes were focused on her boobs. She giggled. "You want to suck them don't you?" He nodded and smiled. "Go on then" and she slid off him and lay back on their bed and she spread her arms out as if to say "They are all yours honey."

He dove down into both, into the cleavage, and he went at them hungrily. He made her instantly horny. She loved how he not only kissed them but licked and sucked both. She loved it more when he licked her nipples and saw each grow to a monstrous size. He always was amazed at how big hers could get but he hadn't been with any other woman in over 19 years and his wife was one of the best looking women around despite their age and despite their were "girls" or much younger women with tighter features then hers.

Out of no where, he went down on her, and before she knew it she was whizzing away as a tongue, his tongue, swirled and dug into her pussy. Her legs were wild. Her body dipped and jumped and heaved mightily as he made her feel orgasmic.

"OHHHH GOD…OH AHHH OOOOHH MMMMM" she yelped loudly. She loved it and he wouldn't stop. Orgasm, he thought. I gotta get her to orgasm. Yes, oh yes…make her orgasm he told himself. "OH…OH…EEHH…OOOOOOHH AHHH YES…OH FUCK YES" she said passionately. "DO ME…MORE OH MORE… OHHHHH MORE HONEY MORE!"

And he dug into her cunt licking it feverishly and fervently. Her ass rose and dropped crazily. Her body twisted and turned and he remained up inside her as he licked the wet and warm depths of her pussy.

Suddenly she screamed so loud that he knew what he heard meant something dramatic. She orgasmed and she came along with repulsive movements throughout her body. Her body went haywire moving in

7

every direction you could fathom. She was getting off on how he did her and seeing as he was hard… He climbed her body.

"God, making love with you is… It's fantastic" he told her.

"I…I know it is" she said adding "and I sure am glad it's with you honey" she told him.

"As opposed to…" he said.

She laughed. He laughed back as he stuck himself inside her. "Don't do it…yet" she said. He lay inside her letting her feel his thickness. "Mmmmmm, I love that" she said. "Ooohh ahhhh that feels soooo…it feels so good sitting in me like that." She took a deep breath of air, her boobs rising high into the air as she swallowed up his cock inside her pussy. "Mmmmm, god you feel mighty."

"Duh…duh…dah" he said.

He didn't know and it almost killed whatever mood was growing between them. Shr brought him down on top of her craning for him to be against her body. She loved how he felt inside her.

Not pumping her madly, they lay together affectionately with his hard cock inside her, and he could feel himself wanting it…wanting to let go all he had for her. She asked him if he wanted to do it now. He said nothing but she knew better.

"Go on and do me…fuck me because I know you want to… I do" she said softly.

And before either knew it he was going off inside her. She loved it. She loved feeling him blowing rampantly inside her. With her eyes closed, she fell in love with her husband all over again. He was by far the greatest man in the world to him.

He knew how to make love and she loved that about him. Afterward, they lay side by side…he was playing with her frothy nipples. He always loved playing with them. She knew it and never stopped him ever.

Afterward, he put his hands around her, pulling her close against him. He could feel her breasts. "Mmmmmm, I still, after all these years, love to hold you, and feel them you know."

"I know" she said with a smile. He couldn't see it. It didn't matter. She liked feeling his arms around her. "What I loved, what I enjoyed…was feeling your cum going crazy inside me."

"Yeah?" he said.

"Uh uhhh" she acknowledged.

"Wanna do it again?" he asked.

"Can you this soon?" she said.

He didn't answer. She knew he couldn't. They'd have to wait a few hours before she'd have to get him horny. He'd have to become hard again and it wouldn't have been as good as it was earlier. Maybe wait a few days before hand.

"I'll wait a few days…then I'm gonna do it right, okay?" she said.

He didn't say a word as he pulled her snugly in against him. Tighter, more lovingly, and as he did he kissed her shoulders and neck. She murmured how she loved it. That's all either one of them needed now. Holding her, kissing her, but feeling those tits… Mmmmm, a woman's tits he thought…never can get enough of them.

Veronica's Hotel

I drove up but slowed down as I approached the parking garage. What am I doing? Is this smart? I want to meet her, I told myself. I do, but I know how these things turn out. They never work. They never do. It always fails. I went around the block again. Why is it I am doing this, I ask myself again. But her emails...those emails of hers... Oh god they were...she is...what she wrote and how she expressed herself in her words...

It drew me, she drew me in. His body heat rose as he thought about his emotions and the Veronica woman he'd only thought about but nothing else until this day. They emailed a couple time before. They were good emails. They were...interesting to put in mildly. She drew me in. I had to meet her. I had to.

Why not? What was the problem with meeting her? That's all. Nothing else. She knows. She knows I like what she thinks I like. I love her words. Yes, that's it. I love how she expresses herself. Man, I feel... more excited. Geez, even my cock's getting hard, or at least a little. Man, I'm rubbing it. Wow, I already think I like her. I've never even met the woman. God, I'm horny? Wow, I'm horny...horny. Can you believe it?

I parked my car but I didn't get out right away. I looked at the piece of paper. I had written it down earlier. Room 309. Turn left, off the elevator. I turned left on floor three. 309... 309... 309. Here, room 309.

The door was open, a little. I stopped, not sure I was sure I wanted to do this. I did but I wasn't sure. At one point I almost opened the door. I didn't. I looked and began thinking about other things. I blew them off. Everything I blew off. I told myself to try it. What the hell.

I knocked and walked in, slowly. She was there. On her bed, the pretty and dark skinned beauty lie there unaware I had stepped inside. Her head was turned away from me. I wanted to say hi but couldn't. Not yet I couldn't. I stared at her...her beauty. I was amazed at how...how pretty she actually was. Dark skinned, tumbling flesh, curves, breasts as perfect as a man, me, would care to have them, and wow was she dressed up.

Not formally, but informally. What was that she had on?

Something…something sexy looking…for me, for us…for me? Oooooooohh mmmmm, I thought. My dick, it tingled. I wanted to rub it. She finally turned my way.

"Oh, hi… Gerald?" she said.

"Yeah, but no one knows that name really" I told her. "Man, wow… Veronica…wow" I began to say or hopefully it came out in a formal sentence.

My body was riveting at the prospects of being against a woman, a real like, and attractive woman who wanted me? Me? Oh…my…god. My heart beat…crazily. I moved to a chair. She was attractive. She really was. Big but beautiful. What was I getting myself into? Was this the right thing to do? Hell yes, I thought. It was. I wanted this again.

Could I satiate her, make her happy? Could I do that?

I sat and we talked, a little, got to know one another, a little. Then she said let's go to the bedroom. My heart ran away. My loins disappeared. What happened? What was going on? Why was I asking all these questions? What did I care?

All we were here for was to take care of those primal needs we both had. "I like you" she told me. "I do. And I love how you write too."

I remember that. I wanted to make love to the young lady, give her body and her all she came for. I hope I could make her happy. I hoped I could. "Wow, I'm going to say something you may… Ohhhhhh wow" I said aloud as I watched her body twirl from left to right, her wide curved derriere swinging to the left and to the right. Can I bite that, I wanted to ask her. May I, I felt like saying. In time, I thought… in good time I will. "You have a great figure" I said.

"Thank you" she said as we turned the corner into the bedroom.

She turned and sat down. I felt my blood pressure sky rocketing. I felt my body going in directions it hadn't gone in a long while… A long, long time. I was nervous. "I want you and need your help doing this… making love to you" I told her. She nodded then smiled. And then she said to me she needed help too. It had been a long time. She's spent way too many days with Mr. V. "Mr. V?" I asked.

"Yes, Mr. V." she said. "My vibrator… It's a great device… a neat and wonderful tool, but it can't…replace the emotional status of a… man, you Stoney. No… No it can't" she said as openly as answering a question in class.

And I had to agree. And I said, "Well let me help you with that project" and that's what I did. "Did you bring it with you?" I asked hoping maybe she had. She said she did. It was in her bag and I hopped up and grabbed it and took it to her. She dug to the bottom of it. Everything we did seemed natural as if it was meant to be. She handed it to me. I never ever had my hands on one, to be honest, and feeling hers was different. I can't explain it but it was.

"Would you like to put it inside me?" she said.

I looked up at her and forced a smile. Really, she knew I did want to do that. I'd love to see her pinkish pussy. I'd love to begin to see her large dark fleshy body; all of it in fact. I would. She was already practically undressed as it was, but her pussy and her ass weren't covered up. Not with those dark panties she had on. Finally, I leaned in and I kissed her on the lips as I pulled away the strap of the panties.

My heart soared. When I looked down and saw it, saw her generous and glorious pussy, everything inside me soared. I beat wildly all over and I felt flushed. I wanted to taste it and taste her too. At that exact moment, I wanted to get instantly horny and slide my hardening cock inside her all too wet cunt, and I wanted to have the greatest sex a man could have with this woman who wanted me that day. But we weren't not ready. Not yet we weren't and she watched me. She watched me as I laid her vibrator down along the seam of her pussy.

Her eyes closed as she felt it, felt me do this womanly thing to her gorgeous pussy. I'd never done anything like it and to do it today to hers was beyond my craziest dreams. I began feeling her soft flesh. Some of it bulged, some of it hung, but none of her ever turned me off. None of her turned me off. I wanted more and more of her. I wanted to hold her, closely. I wanted to know her. I wanted to know all about this dark woman who I allowed to come on to me. We said nothing as we or I did foreplay. I was still dressed from my day at work. Sweater and pants and the rest, I laid by her side feeling her, touching her, and plodding along her bulbous beauty. I fell slowly for a woman I knew nothing about, but I tell you this- It was great and she was great because she watched and smiled as her eyes remained closed, until we kissed.

"I love how you touch my body," she said softly.

What a voice. It was sweet, quiet, and it swallowed me up. "I've never done anything like this" I told her. She asked me what I meant. "Well, I'm pretty old fashioned" I said.

She couldn't believe it based on how I was handling the vibrator, how I was working her pussy. I was gentle and smooth, she told me. She said she loved it on her. That only made me hornier. I wanted to put my cock inside her. She knew that, right? She had to. She smiled and nodded. I looked into her soft eyes. She was a woman of...well you know what I'm going to say...a woman of beauty which I've never encountered before. A woman who came all this way to see me...me I am telling you. It was incredible I was with her, with Veronica Moon today.

Again her soft smooth voice. "Go inside me. Swell inside me. I want to feel you in me."

I looked up. Her eyes, like her voice, were at peace, and I got undressed. I slithered up her body. She inhaled as I did, feeling me,

13

feeling it as it came alive before I even went in her. She oooh'd and she ahhhh'd as I "climbed" over her to put it before her. She said she wanted me and I went in. Inside, she was warm. I didn't want to be violent. No, I didn't and wouldn't be with this woman.

I simply wanted to feel her, be inside her, and do the things a man does with a woman he…he appreciates and likes a lot. I lay there, feeling her insides. Man, it felt good in there. She felt good and the longer I sat inside her, the more I wanted to do this.

We hung on to one another. We held one another. We grabbed one another. I kissed her breasts. They were succulent. They were delicious. Everything about my experience with her, having some of the greatest sex in my entire life with Veronica was and is never going to be forgotten.

I wanted more and more, but once I came and I came deeply inside her core. I came and I enjoyed it. Then I was done. And she held my body closely. I held hers as close. We were warm. It was and an experience I'd never forget, I told myself. Hopefully there would be more of these days.

Beautiful eyes. Beautiful body. Beautiful breast. Great hips. A wonderfully shaped ass. Everything I could ask for from this woman. I love you, I almost said, but knew I didn't.

As time progressed, we came closer. Personally and physically, she and I became closer then any man and any woman can in cases like this. We understood, I thought, each other and I wanted her to know it. Being able to feel a woman's actual naked flesh, hers especially was nothing like I'd ever imagined. I wished I could have stayed longer, but she and I both knew it wasn't possible. I wanted her. Veronica wanted me.

She wanted more then I could ever…ever give of myself. She did not cry when I left three plus hours later. We hugged and it was a long, long hug. We didn't speak, hardly at all. I told her to email me. She said she would. And then she and I kissed. That kiss was a beauty in its own right. Her lips were soft. Her lips were mighty. But I have not forgotten her lips and her kiss, yet. Wow. What a woman.

14

Damon

"That will be $21.95," I said after ringing up his cd.

"Huh? Oh, umm, yeah," he replied seeming to come out of a trance.

I watched him as he fumbled around in his wallet trying to find a credit card. He was a regular customer and I thought he was adorable. He looked about the same height as me at 5'7" with close-cropped brown hair, a five o'clock shadow, and small silver rimmed glasses. He looked kind of rugged and smart at the same time. What made him so adorable, though, was that he seemed to painfully shy. I also got good vibes from him but I wasn't sure if he was interested in me or not.

"Here you go," he said giving me a Visa card.

I looked at the card catching his name, Damon, before running it through the machine. He looked slightly uncomfortable and fidgety as we waited for his card to approve.

"Just sign at the bottom," I said after the receipt finished printing. "Is there anything else you need?" I asked as I took his signed slip from him.

"I was wondering if you could tell me your name?" he asked

"Amanda," I replied smiling.

"That's a nice name."

"Thanks" I said giving him the warmest smile I could.

"Anything else?"

"Umm, I was wondering if we could do something sometime, maybe coffee or something like that?"

"I would love too."

"Uh...you would?" he managed to stammer after a moment of silence.

15

"How about tonight?" I asked. "My shift ends at eleven, if that's not too late."

"No, eleven is okay."

"Why don't I stop by your place after I get off work?" I said. The line of customers behind Damon was getting longer and they were looking impatient. I felt like I had to move things along.

"Alright," he said looking a little shell-shocked. "Um, did you want to go somewhere? I don't what will be open that late."

"Maybe you could have an open bottle of wine waiting for me," I said to him smiling. "I like reds, if that's okay?"

"That sounds great."

He scribbled his name and address down on a post-it note I gave him and handed it to me. His place was right around the corner.

"I'll see you tonight Damon."

"Okay," he said heading toward the door.

I felt my heart beating in my chest as he left the store. I was confident I had him. I felt like I had rocked his world in a good way. He was so shy I felt like I had to be aggressive with him. I liked that. It made me feel like I was in control. I had been worked up for the past few days and had not been able to find a release. For the remainder of my shift, my thoughts dwelled on what I wanted to do with him later that night. It seemed that time was against me but the clock finally said 11pm and I was able to leave.

I found his apartment easily. I hoped he did not have any roommates or at least that they would not be there. I knocked on his door with a sense of anticipation.

"Hi," he said after he opened the door. "Come on in."

"How's it going?" I asked. Looking around it was clear he lived alone.

"Just fine."

"Do you mind if I take a quick shower?" I asked. "It's been a long day at work."

"A shower?" he uttered. "Ugh...Okay. Do you need a towel?"

"That would be great."

"I opened a bottle of wine" he said eagerly as he pulled a towel out the linen closet for me.

"Good, I can't wait to have some."

After he handed me the towel, I went into his bathroom, closed the door, and turned on the water. I took off my clothes and got in the shower enjoying the feeling of warm water flowing over my body. I felt grimy and was glad to get clean. I tried my best not to get my hair wet but it didn't do any good. After I dried off I walked out with the towel wrapped around me.

"Umm Damon, do you have a shirt or something I could put on. I just can't make myself get back into my dirty work clothes."

"Yeah. Sure," he replied. I was rocking his world all right, after reading his expression. "What kind of shirt would you like?"

"I was thinking something like a button up shirt, you know with the long tails hanging down."

"Okay. How about this?"

"Perfect," I replied as he handed me light blue, cotton dress shirt.

I went into the bathroom and put it on making sure to leave a few of the buttons undone. When I came out he was sitting on his couch and I took a seat next to him. He had a bottle of red wine out with two glasses already poured. He handed me one and took one for himself.

We immediately made small talk. He had recently moved up here from Southern California after graduating from UCLA in computer science. He had just taken up a job as a computer programmer in town a few months ago. He also told me that he had been engaged to another woman for most of his years in college. She ended up marrying someone else right before they graduated. He seemed kind of bitter about it but who wouldn't.

"Was she the only woman you've been with?" I asked trying to steer the conversation toward sex. We were each on our second glass of wine and it was clear we were both feeling a little more relaxed.

"No, I mean yes," he said. "She was the only woman I've been with."

"How was she? You know, in bed," I asked. He looked offended at first and I thought he might not answer me.

"She was okay I guess. I definitely enjoyed it more than she did. She didn't like to do it a lot," he finally answered. "So, I suppose you don't have a boyfriend?" Damon asked me clearly trying to change the subject.

"Not really," I replied. "I was kind of seeing someone but I think he's blowing me off."

"I can't believe it," he said. "He's got to be the dumbest guy in the world."

"Why's that?"

"Because you're one of the hottest women I've ever seen."

"Yeah right," I said. "But it's sweet of you to say."

At that moment both I leaned a little closer and kissed him, just a little peck on the lips.

"Do you think your guy would mind that you did that?" he asked teasingly.

"As far as I'm concerned he's not my guy and I don't really care," I answered back. "Besides I want to do much more than that."

"Oh really?"

"Really," I answered looking into his eyes and kissing him again.

I was all over him. I grabbed at his hair as I drove my tongue into his mouth. It took him a few moments but he was soon kissing me back with equal intensity. I felt his hands on my waist and then my hips. I got the sense he wanted to go further but wasn't sure if he should. I took care of that problem by grabbing his hand and putting on my bare ass under my shirt.

He tasted good and I could have kissed him for hours but I had too much pent up lust in me. I could feel his erection under his shorts as I ground myself into him. I became possessed with desire.

"You know," I whispered into his ear as I began kissing his neck. "I've been noticing you for awhile now." I flicked my tongue in his ear making him visibly shiver. "I've wanted you the moment I laid eyes on you. I've imagined you fucking me all day today."

I slid down his body and came to rest on my knees before him. I pulled down his shorts and looked up at him smiling as I pulled out his cock. He threw his head back in pleasure as I began to stroke it softly. I held it in my hand and studied it. It was nice and straight, and just the right size. I let the anticipation build, wanting take him into my mouth.

I pulled his shorts all the way off while he took his shirt off. He looked magnificent sitting back on the couch naked before me. I put a hand on each of his well-muscled thighs and licked the precum off the tip of his hard cock. I ran my tongue over it savoring the masculine taste. I could feel myself getting even more aroused as I took the flesh of his manhood into my mouth. I made his cock all wet with my saliva. Then took his balls in my hand as I slid my lips over his shaft. I felt his pubic hair tickle my noise as my lips reached the base of his cock. I effortlessly took him all the way in to the back of my throat. I felt like I was in the zone and all that existed was my mouth on his cock. The feeling was exquisite. I lost sense of time and was surprised when I heard him breathing faster and moaning louder. I could not get enough of him.

"Oh my god! You're good!" I heard him say between labored breaths. "I've never felt so good."

I did not say anything and just looked up at him making eye contact. I slowly moved my fingers off his balls and massaged his scrotum. I moved further down between his legs and let one of my fingertips graze the rim of his asshole. He did not seem to object, so I continued. I stroked the outside of his hole with my finger. Wet with my saliva I inserted my forefinger inside him ever so slowly. His anus seemed to open up for me and I pushed my finger inside. His moaning gained intensity as I gently rotated my finger inside of him.

"Oh god! I've never felt anything feel so good" he breathed. "You're such a nasty girl."

"Do you like nasty girls?" I asked as I let his cock slip away from my mouth for a moment.

"Oh yes."

"Good."

With that I sucked on him with all the effort I could and I put my finger inside his ass as far as it would go while pressing up against his engorged prostate as hard as I could. He exploded right there with bursts of his cum entering my mouth. It was so intense I could not swallow it all and a lot of it dribbled back down on his cock and my hand that was still stroking him. I milked him dry and licked him clean.

After giving him a moment to recover I climbed up next to him. I planted my lips on his and made him taste himself. He did not seemed to mind and kissed me back enthusiastically.

"You are very nasty," he whispered, as he tasted himself.

"It's my turn now," I said smiling. I saw him look at me and he looked petrified.

"Is everything okay?" I asked.

"Umm, yeah. Everything is fine," he answered smiling. He slid off the couch and we switched positions.

He began kissing the tops of my feet and worked his way up the inside of one of my legs. When he got to the top he went back and started at the bottom of my other leg. When he reached the top again, he unbuttoned my shirt. I sat up and let it fall of my shoulders. He spread my legs slightly and I lifted them up slightly to open myself to him. He began to move in and then stopped.

"I'm sorry," he exclaimed. "I've never done this before and I don't want to mess it up. I want to make you feel the way you made me feel." I felt bad for him. He seemed almost in tears.

"It okay," I assured him. "Just lick around the outside and then gently on my clit," I told him as I outlined, with my finger, where I wanted him lick to me. "When I'm excited you can gently put a finger inside me. I like it when it's twirled around as opposed to in and out. Just be gentle and take your time. Everything will be just fine."

He seemed okay and moved in again. I let out a soft moan as I felt his warm tongue on my sex.

"Oh yes, that's it," I said. "Keep doing that."

My hand clawed at the fabric on the couch as he continued. He slowly licked my pussy from top to bottom. I almost orgasmed right then as I felt his tongue enter my hole. I ran my hands through his hair as I enjoyed his attention. I softly urged him on as he gently spread my lips and put his tongue directly on my clit. I took one of his hands and placed it at my entrance. He took the hint and inserted a finger inside me, gently twirling it around.

"Use two fingers," I whispered. I felt him insert another finger. I was very wet and he had no problem putting it in. Suddenly I pulled his hand away and brought it to my mouth. I looked him in the eye as I licked my juices of his fingers. He resumed his licking and I shifted my hips and pulled my legs farther back.

"Will you do something for me?" I asked.

"Anything," he replied.

"Will you lick me here," I said as I brought my finger down to my asshole.

"Only if you asked nicely," he said smiling.

"Will you lick my ass for me?"

He seemed more confident now, and I liked that. I felt him run his tongue down my swollen sex and then plant kisses around my anus, but not touching it. He teased me like that for what seemed forever. Finally, I felt his warm, wet tongue on my sensitive bud. I rubbed my clit with my finger as his tongue assaulted my backside. He became very aggressive and it was heavenly. His tongue was up and down, back and forth, and then suddenly I felt his tongue penetrate my anus. I felt myself tighten and then relax as he kept pushing further inside.

"Oh yes," I screamed frantically as my finger became a blur over my clit. "Oh fuck! Yes! Oh yeah!"

I spasmed in a massive climax as he kept pushing his tongue deeper into my backside. He then put his mouth on my sex until I finally finished. Right after I pulled up and made him kiss me. I was still hot for it.

"I want you to fuck me now!" I demanded.

He needed no encouragement as he pushed my legs apart and guided his cock into my hole. I almost fainted in pleasure as he slid himself into me. I pulled him close and we kissed, our bodies melding into a slow, steady rhythm. Our chests were pressed together as his hips moved himself in and out of me. Our skin slid together when we began to sweat from our efforts. You could hear the soft sucking sound of my sex grabbing his cock. He then increased his tempo and I laid back looking up at him as he had his way with me. He lowered his face down to my ear and began to whisper nasty little things to me.

"You're a nasty little slut who needs to get fucked," he said.

"Ooooh," I moaned, surprised at his boldness. I grabbed his ass with both hands and pulled him into me. My body started to shutter in orgasm and he responded by pumping me harder. As my orgasm subsided he pulled out and sat up.

"Don't stop," I pleaded. "I don't care if you cum inside me. Just fuck me."

"You're sure, because I'm about to blow."

"You should do me from behind?"

"Bend over," he said.

I rolled over and pushed myself up onto my hands and knees thrusting my ass up in the air. I brought my hand to my clit and he pushed his cock back inside me. I tossed my head back and moaned loudly as I felt him enter me.

"Oh yeah, Fuck me nice as hard."

He grabbed onto my hips and drove himself into me, filling me with his cock. I felt his finger between my ass cheeks. I moaned letting him know that I was okay with that. I felt his finger slide into my asshole and then clamped my anus down on his finger. It was really turning me on. His finger moved in and out of my backside as he continued to fuck me.

"You make me feel so nasty," I told him.

"Sorry," he replied.

"No! I think it's fuckin' hot feeling like this. I love being nasty."

"Then how would you like to have my cock up your ass then my nasty slut."

"Mmmm yeah, I thought you would never ask." He pulled out and I rolled onto my back.

"I like it this way," I said pulling my knees up to my chest.

I made him find some lube which did not take long. "Go slowly," I said as I felt him apply the lube.

He pressed his lubed covered head up against my hole. I made myself relax as he pushed forward. My breathing became faster at the intensity of the sensation. It felt good but it was so intense I almost could not take it. He slowly worked his way in very patiently. Eventually he was able to move himself all the way in and out of my ass.

"I don't know how long I'm going to last," he warned.

"No, no, no, no. Don't cum yet," I pleaded. "Keep fucking me. Keep fucking my ass. Just long enough for me to cum again. You can cum anyway you want to after that."

I felt myself loosening up a bit, and he started to fuck me harder. I clenched my ass around his cock and I fingered my clit.

"Oh yeah, just like that," I moaned as he went at me hard and fast. "Oh my god! Yes! Oh! I'm gonna cum!"

With that I came hard, moaning and twitching in pleasure. He pulled out right after I was done. After I recovered for few moments I sat up.

"Lay down," I told him.

He complied, slumping back on the couch. I pushed his knees up towards his head. I lowered my head and ran my tongue across his balls, then going lower and lower.

"Oh fuck," I heard him say as I my tongue poked at his asshole.

24

He placed a hand on my head as I licked his most private area, running my tongue in circles as I stroked his cock. He suddenly sent massive spurts of cum into the air landing on his chest. I immediately wrapped my lips around his pulsing cock, filling my mouth with his cum. When he finally stopped firing I released him and crawled up next to him, licking the creamy liquid off his chest.

"Damn!" he said. "You are a nasty girl."

I just smiled at his comment. We got up and we to his bed falling asleep in each other's arms. We went on a cycle of sex and sleep every couple of hours until the afternoon of the next day. We've hooked up several times after that on the weekends, repeating the events of that night.

The Girl's Bathroom

"So, where's the weirdest place you've done it?" I heard Dan ask. I didn't know how we got into the topic of our sexual histories when we were supposed to be studying for a chemistry exam we had the next morning, but I didn't mind. Studying was getting tedious, and this was fun, not to mention arousing. I looked around the library to see if anyone else had heard Dan's question. It was late on a Sunday night, and there were not many people around.

"I guess it would have to be on the hood of a car in the parking lot of my high school during homecoming," I replied after I was convinced no one was eavesdropping. While I recalled the experience in my mind, I felt myself getting more turned on, and become acutely aware of my physical attraction to Dan. "How about you? Where's the weirdest place you've done it?"

"Ugh, I've only done it in a bed," He finally replied after not answering for a long time. I smiled at him as I saw him blush; I didn't mean to embarrass him. I could feel my not so innocent desires beginning to take control.

"Why don't we change that?" I said to him with a smile. It was my turn to blush now.

"What?"

"Come on let's do it in the bathroom right now. There's hardly anyone around. No one will catch us." He just looked at me with a stunned expression, and I thought for a moment or two that he might not go for it.

I hadn't been with a guy since I broke up with my exboyfriend a few months before. I was very attracted to Dan, and had been fantasizing about being with him since the first day of school when we met. He stood around 6'2", and was kind of skinny. He had short sandy blonde hair, and I thought he was a good-looking guy. He was 19, and your typical young male.

I felt relieved when he finally smiled, and started packing up his books. I took his hand and lead him to the girl's bathroom, in the back corner. No one was around. We put down our backpacks, and went into a stall locking the door.

There was an awkward silence at first, so I kissed him. It was so nice to have his lips finally against mine. I felt his hands roaming down my back and then affixing themselves on my ass. After awhile I reached down and unzipped his pants. He was half erect when I took him in my mouth. He got fully hard quickly.

I pulled off my panties from underneath my skirt, hanging them on a hook inside the stall. He sat on top of the toilet with the lid closed, and his pants around his ankles. I faced him and then straddled his lap. He was kind of big, and I thought since it had been so long for me that I might not be ready for him.

However, I was really wet at this point, mostly from the novelty of my blatant proposition to Dan. I wrapped my hand around his member and guided him toward my entrance. I moaned in exquisite pleasure as he easily slide inside my wet sex. It had been too long. I rode him, grinding my clit against his pubic bone.

Surprisingly, I came only after a few minutes. I wanted to moan loudly, but I made myself silent as possible not wanting anyone to hear us.

After I calmed down from my climax, I pulled myself off of him telling him we should change positions. He was going to have to do the work the rest of the way. I stood over the toilet with my hands against the back wall. He entered me from behind. God, his cock felt so good filling up from behind like that. He pumped away, pushing himself in and out of me. He lifted up my blouse and gently pinched my nipples as he fucked me in the bathroom stall. Starting to feel excited again, I reached between my legs, and began to touch myself while he pounded me.

When I heard the bathroom door open I thought he would stop not wanting to get caught, but he just kept on going. I could hear the person's footsteps and another stall door open. I felt my excitement level kick up a notch knowing there was someone right next to us. Then, suddenly, Dan began grunting and moaning. He was going shoot his load with someone else in the bathroom.

I continued to finger my clit with more force. Dan grabbed onto my hips, pulling me completely into him as he came inside me. Just as he was finishing, I had my second orgasm. We just stood there, with Dan's arms wrapped around me, trying to catch our breath. In the meantime we heard the person leave the stall then using the sink to wash her hands. If she had heard something, then she didn't let on, but I figured there was no way she couldn't have. Once she left, we started giggling hysterically.

I spent most of that night at Dan's apartment, and needless to say, I was sore the next morning.

Gerald

I sat on the couch thinking shouldn't have had so much to drink. I didn't know whose house I was in, but whoever lived there had thrown a great party. I had spent the night dancing, drinking, and generally having a good time. Now, however, it was getting late, and a lot of people had left. When Gerald saw me on the couch he came over and sat next to me.

Gerald and I were dating I suppose. We had shared a chemistry class, and had ended up sleeping together within the first month we met. I wouldn't have called us boyfriend and girlfriend; we were more like sex buddies.

We hung out together, but mostly to have sex. He had heard about this party, and invited me along. We both knew what would be coming later, and I was looking forward to it. We had already done it once, earlier that afternoon in his apartment, but I knew we would do it again when we got back his place.

He kissed me, and we started making out on the couch. I felt his hand make its way along my inner thigh under my dress. I wasn't wearing panties or a bra per his request. His fingers gently caressed the outer folds of my vagina getting me wet. He knew how to touch me, and he was getting me hot. I was kind of drunk, and didn't care if anyone was looking our way, they would have known what Gerald was doing to me.

When I finally did see a guy or two peeking at us, I assumed they had got an eye full.

"I want to see you do another guy," I heard Gerald whisper in my ear.

"What?"

"I want to see you with another guy!"

"Another guy?" I said surprised. "Where did that come from?"

29

"I don't know," Gerald said. "I've just been imagining you with other guys,
and it kind of turns me."

Gerald had caught me off guard and I didn't really know what to say.
"Who?"
I finally said even more surprised than before that I was even
entertaining the thought.

"Him," he said pointing across the room. "He said he would."

"You already asked him?" I said indignantly.

"Don't be upset," Gerald said. "If you don't want to, that's totally okay,
but I figured it wouldn't be a big deal since you had told me your
fantasy about taking on multiple guys. I think it would be totally
hot!"

I had to admit the thought was erotic, and it was true that I've had a
long time fantasy of having more that one guy at a time. With my
inhibitions suppressed from my alcohol consumption along with
feeling
horny this seemed like a golden opportunity.

"Okay," I told him.

He looked a little surprised at my quick agreement, but then quickly
became excited. He took my hand and lead me a bedroom. Once inside
he
closed the door and kissed me. I felt him unzip the back of my dress,
and pull it off of me. I stood there naked in a pair of black heels. I
was a nervous with anticipation, but turned on at the same time.

"Wait here," he said to me as I laid back on the bed.

A few moments after he left the room the door reopened. I saw the
silhouette of three guys, and one of them was Gerald. He didn't tell
me
he wanted to see me with two other guys.

I saw them undressing, but the room was dark so it wasn't that easy to tell who was who. One of the guys approached the bed, and laid down next to me. We began kissing and his unfamiliar body felt nice against mine. As we continued making out, I felt him grind his hardened manhood against my thigh. Then he broke off our kiss and started to kiss me all over.

He gently sucked on my nipples and went down on me for a while. I was really nervous and had trouble getting into it at first. Just when I was starting to relax and enjoying it he stopped and climbed on top of me.

Luckily, I was really wet at this point and he entered me easily. I didn't know if it was nerves or what, but I felt detached from the whole thing. I had let this strange man enter me, but I was somewhat disappointed that I didn't feel more.

Then all the sudden he quickened his pace, and it was all I could do to hang onto him.

As his friend pounded me into oblivion caught Gerald's eye. I could just make out the expression on his face as he watched me getting fucked by his friend. He seemed to be enjoying the show and even gave me the thumbs up sign.

Keeping my eye contact with down I found myself getting really excited. It was a total turn on having Gerald watch me getting thoroughly fucked by this guy whose name I didn't know. I moaned loudly as I climaxed.

This seemed to get to Gerald's friend as he began to moan and grunt, filling me up with his semen, while I was in the middle of my orgasm. I wasn't disappointed knowing I still had two guys to go.

As soon as first guy got up off the bed, the other guy replaced him. As he climbed on top of me I could see his hard cock swinging out in front of him. It had a big upward curve, unlike any other cock I had ever seen.

I could feel the cum from the first guy dripping down my crotch as the second guy took a hold of my legs and held them straight up in the air. I looked down between my legs I saw the guy guiding the tip of his head at my already once used pussy. He gave his hips a little forward move and he slipped right inside me.

"Oh Yes! Fuck me!" I moaned.

He fucked me so fast it was like he was in a race. His cock was driving in and out of me hard and fast. I was having a difficult time keeping up with his deep, fast pounding. He felt so different from the previous guy.

He continued to fuck me harder and faster. I could hear the bed banging up against the wall. Then, all at once, he pushed as hard and deep inside me as he could.

"I'm cumming," he grunted.

Then his body writhed about while he continued to move himself in and out of me in erratic strokes while he pumped his hot cum deep inside me.

When he was finally done we laid there for a few moments in a sweaty heap while he caught his breath. He seemed to forget we weren't alone in the room, but then suddenly remembered. I could feel his cum running out of me after he pulled out and climbed off of me.

"Get on your hands and knees," I heard the first guy say.

I looked down at him and was surprised to see him fully hard again. The other guy had finished so fast that I was still hot for it and did as asked, getting on my hand and knees.

He got behind me and took a hold of my hips. In one move I was full with his cock again. He was a bit larger than the previous guy. He bent over a little and took both of my breasts into his hands and played with my nipples just the way I like as he fucked me from behind. He wasn't going as fast as the previous guy, so I was able to keep up with him as he moved himself in and out of me.

"Don't stop," I moaned as I finally began to feel another orgasm coming on. "That feels so good."

"Cum with me," he moaned as he started to pick up speed.

In a short time he was fucking me like a madman. I moved to his rhythm,
pushing my hips back to meet his thrusts.

Oh yes!" I yelled as we fucked wildly. "Fuck me! Oh yes! God yes!"

"Here it comes," he grunted.

He pushed himself all the way inside me and I pushed back on his cock.

We both came at the same time for the second time that night. I could feel his cock exploding inside me as I convulsed in orgasm. I flexed the muscles of my sex trying to milk every drop of cum out of him.

"You liked that, didn't you?" He asked me as he playfully slapped my ass.

"Oh God yes, I loved it," I said falling flat on my stomach. His cock made a loud sucking noise as it popped out of me. I could feel his hot sperm running back out the entrance of my sex. I could see him cleaning off his cum sticky cock with the edge of the sheet.

"We'll have to do this again," one of the guys said, as they got dressed.

"It's a date," I replied. They each gave me a kiss goodbye and they left the room.

As soon as the door closed Gerald got on the bed and gave me a big hug and
kiss.

"That was wild," he said. "You totally came that last time, didn't you?"

"Maybe, a little," I said smiling, slightly embarrassed.

"Yeah, a little. From what I saw, you came a lot," he said kissing me again.

Then I felt his hand play with my still hard nipple for a few seconds before feeling it move down my body.

"Oh my God!" he said fingering my sex. "I've never felt you this wet. Oh fuck does this feel good. I never dreamed you would feel so hot filled with other guys' cum."

Suddenly in one fast move, Gerald was on top of me lining up his hard cock at then entrance of my cum filled hole. Very slowly he pushed himself inside me.

"Oh God, does this feel good!" he said breathlessly once he was in as far as he could go. He moved himself in and out of a few times before he moaned, "Oh fuck! I'm cumming!"

I had never seen Gerald cum so fast before. I heard him grunt and moan as he penetrated me as deeply as he could while he pumped me with his seed. He collapsed on top of my as soon as he was done. "God Amanda, I'm sorry. It just felt so good. I had to cum."

"That's okay," I said laughing. "I'm glad you enjoyed this as much as I did."

"Oh, I did," he said. "I just can't believe how good it feels to be inside you." Gerald began moving hips really slow, and soon after he was hard again.

"Oh I think little Gerald is coming back alive," I said.

"I just can't stop fucking you."

In less than a minute Gerald was fully hard again and pounding me with his full force. I was just as turned on as Gerald at this point. The idea that I was lubricated with the cum of three different guys as

Gerald fucked me it drove me wild. I think I was wetter than I had ever been in my life up to that point.

Gerald's hard cock fucked me as hard and fast as he could. I locked my legs around him as we continued to fuck like wild banshees. My poor little pussy was making loud sucking sounds with each of Gerald's thrusts.

"Don't stop," I begged. "Oh God, don't stop! Fuck me harder! Fuck me harder dammit! Don't stop!" Faster he went with long hard strokes that were drove me over the top. "I'm cumming," I screamed. I writhed around in pleasure as Gerald continued to pound me as hard as he could. My orgasm was so intense that it made the room spin.

"I'm cumming!" Gerald announced. He drove his cock deep inside me and exploded. "Oh God, Amanda," he moaned as he added more to cum to that which had already been dumped inside me.

We got dressed and Gerald drove us back to his place. As I sat in his car, it felt like a river of cum was running out of me, which soaked the material of my dress.

When we got to Gerald's place I immediately slipped out of my cum soaked dress and crawled into bed. I passed out a few minutes afterward. An hour or so later I was awakened with Gerald fucking me once again in the wee hours of the morning.

We ended up doing it a couple of more times before we finally got out of bed the next day. Each time he would go on about hot it had been watching me fuck his friends and how good it had felt to fuck me after they had cum inside me.

I could hardly walk the next day, and it took me a few days to fully recover. That night had definitely pushed me to my limits, but I was ready to do it again. I just hope Gerald is up doing it again.

Afternoon Delight

It was a hot August afternoon, and I was spending the day lying out by the pool. The heat was intense, and there was nothing much else I wanted to do in the 100+ degree heat. I was half asleep when I heard the phone ring next to me.

"Hello?"

"Hey. What are you doing tonight?" I heard Steve ask.

"Nothing," I replied.

"Good, I wanted to see you tonight," he said. "I was wondering if you would like to watch some videos with some friends of mine?"

"Sure," I said. He told me to be there around 7:30.

I had been dating Steve for couple of months. I wasn't sure if we were serious or not, but he did call me his girlfriend. We had met at a party where ended up naked in a walk-in closet for a couple of hours.

Afterward we exchanged phone numbers, and had seen each other two or three times a week. I had not really met any of his friends yet; so hanging out with them would be unusual.

After I ate dinner I took a shower, put on pair of shorts and a tank top, and then drove over to Steve's apartment. One the way over I wondered what type of movies he and his friends had rented. Probably total guy movies with lots of shooting and death. 'Oh well,' I thought to myself.

At least I will get to see Steve; I had been itching to see him. Lying out in the sun all day had made me horny, and I couldn't wait to be with him.

I found a parking spot in Steve's apartment complex, and went to his door. I heard music coming from the apartment as I knocked on the door. There was no answer, so I let myself in.

I smiled as I entered the room, and dropped my purse on a chair by the door. I saw Steve, said hello and give him a big kiss letting him know what I wanted later that night. He playfully groped my ass as I tasted the beer on his lips.

I went to the kitchen and find a wine cooler, and saw the movies sitting on the kitchen table. I checked them out curious to know what we were going to watch that night. There was a Wesley Snipes action flick, and another movie called "Erotic Liaisons." That's when I noticed Steve and his friend looking at me nervously.

"What?" I asked.

"Umm, you kind of weren't supposed to see that movie on the table," Steve told me in a meek voice.

"Don't worry about it," I said smiling. "Who knows, I might like it."

I suddenly saw relief in their expressions.

"By the way, Amanda. This is Tom, a good friend of mine."

"Nice to meet you Tom," I said as I shook his hand.

"Likewise," he replied.

He was a good-looking guy, but he was kind of smarmy. I could only imagine what he had been thinking when he looked me up and down.

The three of us settled into the main room. I sat with Steve on the couch, and Tom sat on a nearby chair. Two hours or so later the Wesley Snipes movie was done, and I was on my fourth wine cooler. I had quite a buzz going, and felt my inhibitions dropping away.

I was kind of hoping Tom would go home so that Steve could take me to bed, but the way they had carried on it didn't seem like that would happen anytime soon.

"So, are we going to see the second movie?" I asked more to get a reaction out of them than anything else. Tom and Steve just looked at each other not knowing what to say. "What? You don't think I'll like it?"

"I don't know," Steve replied. "We just don't want you to feel uncomfortable or anything."

As I got up off the couch, I could feel Tom's eyes on me. I picked the movie off the kitchen table and popped it into the VCR. I also grabbed a couple or beers and a wine cooler from the fridge, tossing the beers to Tom and Steve.

I snuggled up to Steve as the movie started. The screened showed two women going at it while the opening credits rolled. I giggled to myself wondering what I was in for.

It was basically a mild porno, and as it continued I could tell that Steve was getting turned on. I snuggled a little more into him with one hand on his shoulder and the other on his chest.

I slipped myh and down toward his short and then up his shirt feeling his bare chest under my palm. I planted a light kiss on his neck, and out of the corner of my eye I noticed Tom discreetly glancing at us.

Feeling uninhibited from the alcohol I lifted Steve's shirt over his shoulders. He helped me out by taking off his shirt. I grazed my nails over his chest, and I noticed that Tom was watching us. Steve turned toward me, and I faced him as I straddled his lap.

We kissed deeply and I buried my tongue deep into his mouth. At of the corner of my eye I noticed that we had Tom's full attention. I pushed my crotched against Steve's feeling hard on underneath his shorts.

"Take me here, right now," I whispered into Steve's ear.

He hesitated for a moment, glancing at Tom, and I kissed him again. Then I suddenly felt Steve's hands on my thighs, sliding them over my ass, and finally underneath my tank top. I wasn't wearing a bra, and his fingers quickly made there way to my nipples.

He squeezed them ever so gently just the way I like, and I immediately felt the wetness building between my legs. My hands roamed over Steve's bare muscular torso.

I nuzzled his neck, planted kisses on his chest, and finally took one of his nipples into my mouth. I heard him moan in pleasure and his grinding against me became more urgent.

I sat up and pulled my shirt off and I felt his chest against mine after I pulled him close to kiss him again. I glanced over at Tom again and I saw him turn his turn away quickly pretending to watch the movie.

He looked a little uncomfortable. I had initially thought that he might be turned on watching us, and I felt kind of bad that he wasn't.

However, it just felt so good that I didn't want to stop. I continued to look at Tom and I smiled at him when we made eye contact. That time he didn't turn away. I thought it was so hot as I watched him watch me with Steve.

I felt Steve unbutton my shorts, and stood up so that he could pull them down off of me. He had taken off both my shorts and panties, so that when I returned to Steve's lap I was naked. I looked over at Tom and saw that he was still watching us. I smiled at him again and he smiled back that time.

"Take off your shorts," I whispered to Steve.

I laid back on the couch and spread my legs as I waited for Steve. I noticed Tom hadn't taken his eyes off of me, and he saw staring with his mouth open. Steve, naked and hard, got on top of me, and the feeling of his body against mine is exquisite. We writhed around together enjoying the sensations of our naked bodies rubbing up against each other.

When I felt his manhood rub up against my wet sex I repositioned myself and suddenly felt the tip of his cock enter my well-lubricated pussy. Like a predator getting his kill, his cock impaled me in one strong stroke. He filled me up, and he began to move himself in and out of me.

With Steve facing the other way I looked over at Tom again. Our eyes locked as his friend fucked me harder and harder. I wanted him to watch me and get off on it, and he didn't disappoint. I moaned in pleasure when I felt the beginnings of an orgasm coming on.

"Take me from behind," I whispered lustily into Steve's ear.

I got on my hands and knees facing towards Tom's chair. Steve mounted me from behind, and his cock founded the entrance to my pussy once again. I felt him fill me up from behind, and he quickly began to move in and out of me. Tom continued to watch, and we locked eyes again. The room started to spin when Steve reached between my legs and began to rub my clit while he continued to fuck me senseless from behind.

"Oh God! I'm Cumming!" I yelled as I felt my orgasm pulse through me.

It took over every ounce of my body, making me writhe in pleasure, and Tom watched me intently the whole time. I continued to moan as I fully enjoyed the sensations of my climax. Just as I was coming down I heard Steve moan as he came filling me up with his seed.

Steve collapsed on top of me when he finished, and I just lay there basking in the afterglow. After a few minutes I began to feel uncomfortable underneath Steve's weight. When he didn't move after I asked him to get off of me, I figured out that he had fallen asleep.

When I finally maneuvered myself out from under him I couldn't believe he was still asleep. As I stood there I suddenly remembered that Tom is still in the room. He had his shorts pulled down and was stroking himself. He kept going when I noticed what he was doing.

Iwassomewhat fascinated and he seemed to enjoy me watching him so I sat on the coffee table in front of Tom's chair and just watched him. It wasn't often I got to see a guy masturbate.

He took off his shirt, pulled his shorts down all the way, making himself naked, and continued to pleasure himself in front of me. I began to touch myself as sort of a show at first, but I became more and more turned on as I continued.

"Cum for me," I whispered to Tom hoping he would finish quickly before Steve woke up.

"Can I cum on you?" he asked.

I could tell that he wanted to really bad, but I was starting to get nervous that Steve would wake up and see us. I didn't think Steve would be into his friend spurting all over me. I didn't really answer him and continued to sit on the coffee table touching myself. I suppose Tom took my silence as a yes because he stood up began stroking himself with his cock aimed at straight at me.

"I want you to cum again," I heard him say.

I was still nervous that Steve would wake up, but I was really turned on. Tom's muscle toned body looked good, and there was something primal about the way he was touching himself. I uttered a low moan as

I felt my sex gushing like a river while I began to massage my clit with more enthusiasm. I watched him stroke his cock right in my face as he watched me masturbate. When I sensed he was close I began to play with myself at a more frantic space.

All the sudden my second orgasm crashed through my body, and I bit the inside of my cheek to stifle my involuntary moans. Just as I was finishing I heard Tom grunt and moan louder and I saw him tense up. I watched his warm fluid spray from his cock onto my chest and stomach as I continued to climax.

Watching him like that was very erotic.

As soon Tom was done I was relieved to see that Steve was still asleep.Tom and I just sat there for a few minutes staring at each other.

"That was hot," he said.

"Yeah, it was," I agreed. "But this is gonna be our little secret."

"I totally agree."

"You should get dressed before Steve wakes up and sees us like this," I said standing up.

My knees were a little shaky and I grabbed onto Tom's shoulder for support. He reached out and put his hand on my stomach, rubbing his cum into my skin. It felt good and I didn't stop him right away. Then both of his hands moved up to my breasts as he continued to rub his fluid into my skin. I still didn't make him stop until we both turned toward Steve when we heard him stir.

"I'm going to the bathroom to clean up," I said. "You should really go."

"I know," he said picking gathering up his clothes up from the floor. "But I just can't get enough of you, besides you seem pretty into it too."

"That's beside the point," I said. "I don't want Steve to wake up."

"I don't either," Tom said following me into the bathroom.

He locked the door behind us and we just kind of stood there in the bathroom awkwardly staring at each other naked.

"You look so good I could eat you," he said pulling me close to him and putting his mouth on one of my nipples.

I didn't pull away as he started to lick his cum off my body. I wanted to tell him to stop, worried that at any moment Steve would wake up and want to use the bathroom, but I just couldn't make myself. It felt really good and I just kept thinking a little bit longer, just a little longer.

The next thing I knew I was sitting on the bathroom counter with Tom kneeling on the floor between my legs going down on me. He knew what he was doing and it was all I could do to keep myself quiet. I wanted to scream in pleasure, but I kept as quiet as I could still worried about Steve walking in on us.

I grabbed onto Tom's head with my hands as I climaxed once again. I couldn't breath as the waves of pleasure flowed through me. Eventually I had to push Tom away when I became too sensitive.

"I've always wanted to do that," I heard him say I sat there trying to catch my breath.

"What's that?" I asked.

"Eat out a girl who'd just been fucked by another guy."

"You're a nasty boy, huh?" I said enjoying his naughtiness.

"Yeah, I guess so," he said seeming embarrassed.

"Don't worry," I said standing up and grabbing onto his semi-erect manhood. "I like boys who are a little on the nasty side." I continued to stroke him until he was fully hard. "Fuck me," I said as I sat up on the counter once again.

He was long, hard, and more than ready. He grabbed onto my hips as he moved between my legs. I grabbed onto his member guiding him toward me. I felt the tip of his head outside my wet sex, and then he was slipping inside me.

He thrust his hips, clutched my ass, and pulled me towards him forcing himself all the way inside me. I had given myself to the moment. I didn't care if Steve walked in on us or not, all I wanted was for Tom to fuck me senseless.

"Oh God, you're so wet," Tom whispered. "This feels so good."

"I know," I said my voice coming out breathy.

He drew himself out, part way, then in, and after that there was nothing but his body inside mine. He thrust into me as hard as he could and the sound of flesh hitting flesh punctuated every thrust of his body.

Sounds emanated from my throat, by the sheer force of it, and from the sensations as he moved in and out of me. My body opened up to him as he thrust himself in and out of me over and over again.

I heard his breathing quicken, his thrusts take on an urgency, harder,faster, until he cried out, and still he didn't stop. As I felt his swelling warmth spill inside me,

I felt my body contract, jerking. I was unable to control it and wrapped my arms around him, holding his sweat-covered body against mine. He leaned into me, his hands still grabbing onto the cheeks of my ass, his head leaning on my shoulder, I could hear him grunt and moan into my ear until he finally finished.

We sat there with him still inside me for a long time.

"Thank you," he said in a ragged whisper, finding his voice first.

"It was my pleasure."

I felt stiff and sore as he slowly pulled himself away from me. Then we both looked up in alarm as we heard Steve walking down the hallway.

"You sneak out while I distract him," I said.

I turned off the light and intercepted Steve in the hallway.

"It's about time you woke up," I said to him. "I'm not done with you yet," I continued as I began to fondle him.

It didn't take much persuading to get Steve interested, and I lead Steve straight to the bedroom and onto the bed.

"You're really slippery," Steve commented as he entered me. "I must have lubed you up from before."

I could only laugh to myself, and began to wonder what the consequence of what I had done with Tom would be. I was surprised I didn't feel guilty, and I actually still felt slightly euphoric over the whole thing.

Just as I started to focus on my sex with Steve, and I starting getting into it, he began to cum emptying himself inside me for the second time that night. I fell asleep wondering, not if, but when I would be with Tom again.

The Carpenter

They thought he was acting like a child or a real good looking teenager for that matter. He was standing there, ogling almost all of them. Looking at women, young and old alike and as he watched them he'd find a way to get down on his knees, trying somehow to look up their skirts, if they had one on.

They were right of course. He was doing that but at the same time what they didn't know was he was also, somehow, getting engagements and dates in one way or another with many of them. Some were around his age but most appeared to be much older. Their thoughts were that regardless of his actions he was young and healthy, but he was the most handsome young man they'd seen in a long while. He was well built and his personality made up for it all most thought. That's how it all began for them.

"So you…do carpentry?" one after another would ask him throughout the afternoon. "Really… But you're not working right now at all?" He'd look them right in the eyes and smile. He'd say no in his soft toned expression. That did it for them. "Well to be honest" one went on to tell him… "I actually have a couple projects you could do at my place." She gazed back into his gentle eyes. "I guess…I could have you come over and" and she found her heart fluttering as she said it "and do some of them at my house. I mean… That's if you're interested of course."

It almost seemed as if they were standing in line for him as he "left" and came back. He brought out his "book." He wrote down their name and their phone number as well. He'd speak with them and write down other notes. He'd stand there and even write down what they looked like. They didn't know it and it was fine with him. He loved the older women. He enjoyed their company a lot. He thought the older ones would appreciate him and his personality too.

"I'll call you?" he'd say in the kind and almost alluring tone of voice.

They'd smile as their eyes simultaneously checked him out. One would say "Of course" or "Yes" or "Come over whenever." Another was telling him "Great, we'll work something out soon, right?"

45

The first one...the oldest one...was for him...magnificent. Medium shoulder length hair, she was as mature as any woman might be. Her smile and her eyes were killer features, he thought, and for this 25 year old out of work carpenter...he was ready. Many men felt the same way about her too. She wasn't the aggressor like he expected her to be but she was in fine, fine shape. With her big enough boobs and those mature womanly curves, she easily got him over to her home to "work" on it.

She smelled nice as heck as well as she was dressed to the "nines" that morning. In a casual top and skirt, her eyes glowed. Her lips impressed him too but the question on his mind was...what was it she really wanted? Passion, sex, kissing....ohhh and down inside those thighs? Did she want me to undress her and take hold of her? Did she need me to kiss her thick and sexy lips too? She had to be well over 35, maybe even 40 he thought, but he wasn't sure. He tried to dispel what many men thought of her as he evaluated it all.

"Well Mrs. Hampton...you sure look...nice today?" he tried to say in a confident voice.

"Jarrod" she replied "that's a nice thing to say."

She wore her smile so well he wanted to stop everything he was doing and turn and look her in the eyes. He wanted to "stare" her down telling her he'd do anything to be with her. He wanted to walk up to her and take her hand and lead her somewhere private. He wanted to gaze into her eyes as one hand slowly reached beneath her dress and felt those silky thighs of hers.

He wanted to caress the insides of them when she least expected it too. He was ready. He was sure she was. Why else would she invite him over? Was he too close to her? No, he wasn't too close. Then it happened. He noticed it almost immediately. Her eyes seemed to float about him as she ogled his manly features as if to tell him "Go on, do it. Feel the insides of my thighs. Feel me all over down there... Do it Jarrod. I need this badly honey."

So he did it. He reached down to her skirt's bottom and lifted it up. She jumped back. "JARROD...WHAT...WHAT ARE YOU DOING?" she abruptly said. She had no idea he'd do that.

None whatsoever but he had and when she abruptly said what she had, he pulled away, quickly. He didn't want any misinterpretation but he caused it. She asked him why he did what he had. He didn't answer. She asked again but knew she wanted it to happen. She just didn't tell him. They looked at one another. She could still feel his hand inside her thighs.

Ohhh, do that again Jarrod she told herself. Do it again. It felt so...so good. I want that to happen again. I so want it to happen, don't you? Do me like that again, honey. I just wasn't expecting it to happen like that. Ohhh and kiss me too...kiss me first. Then slip that hand of yours inside my thighs.Yes dear... I'm in shape. My legs...they are...tight and strong and firm. Yes, they should be silky and soft for you, she'd told herself... So do it...just do it... Kiss my lips...ohhh god yes honey...do it...but kiss me on my lips first. Then do your thing. That's all she was thinking as she looked him in his eyes.

Kiss my lips baby...kiss them hard.

He didn't. He was too inexperienced for that. "Jarrod... Stop" she told him, passion filling her body all over... "Please stop, will you?" She looked at him. He looked stupid standing in front of her wanting what he wanted. "I want you. I do. I want you badly, but what I want, first and foremost, is a soft passion filled kiss on my lips. Every woman, every girl does. Once I have that...then we'll see...okay sweetheart?"

He understood, kind of, and with that he looked into the older attractive woman's eyes and did it flawlessly. He took hold of her body, perfectly. He brought himself closer to her body and with his natural abilities he kissed her mightily on her lips. She was impressed as hell. HE COULD KISS. He could really kiss too. Wow, she thought. This man...he surely knew how to kiss a woman and he kissed her hard. He didn't let up. His tongue slowly found its way into her mouth and it waggled inside feverishly.

Her body weakened as it did. She wanted him more and more, but he continued to kiss her mouth, her lips. His tongue naturally went wild as she let him do his thing. His hands held her closely and intimately.

Placed against her back, she felt one, then two of them pulling at her soft shapely ass as the front of her body instantly pushed against the front of his. His cock, buried beneath his jeans, was hard, and with that he knew he needed it all out of her. He pushed harder. She felt the need and with the way he was passionately kissing her lips, she pushed against his body hard too.

They stopped. She looked into his eyes. She smiled. Then she spoke. "Now...that is how you get a woman...interested in you...if there's anything going to happen between them."

And with that she smiled some more as she looked into his eyes. Before he knew it her top rolled off the top of her head. Before he knew it, he was staring at her gorgeous and sexy bra. Before he knew it, her body seemed to be moving in his direction. Before he knew it, her hands took hold of his... And before he knew it, his hands were all over her boobs.

"Now...feel me. Touch this...and feel it" she said as her eyes closed.

He looked into her face and saw her closed eyes. He felt her bra covered boobs. He rubbed and caressed and teased her upper body and especially her bosoms. He leaned in although she didn't expect it and he kissed her cleavage, but before she knew it he was removing the straps of her bra off her shoulders and sliding her bra off her shoulders. She wasn't stopping him so he went all the way. It lie beneath her boobs. They were...so full, he told himself. His cock raged on. He wanted his jeans undone and off his body. He wanted at least a hand on it and stroking it. He so wanted her warm and tender hand doing something to his body.

"I want you" he told her.

"And we'll get there...honey" she replied.

With that he leaned in and kissed her breasts. He kissed them and he kissed hard, all over. She loved how his lips felt on them and pushed herself into his mouth forcing him to kiss them endlessly it seemed. He heard her breathing more rapidly while kissing them all over. Finally, he took hold of her and gradually they lay down on the carpeted floor. He kissed not only her breasts but her lips again as well as around her neck and shoulders.

This guy is good, she thought. God is he ever, she told herself as he kissed her upper body. He looked at her as if trying to get a read on her telling him that he was doing it all correctly. It seemed he was seeing as she had a smile on her and wasn't moving. Her arms and hands were against his body pulling him towards hers.

"Do...you know...how...horny I am?" he asked.

"Yes...I can feel it" she appeared to say warmly.

"Do you want me to take off my pants then?"

"Not yet...just keep kissing me" she replied.

So that was what he did. He kept kissing the woman, passionately, but he tired of it shortly after that. He wanted to get off. He wanted to be naked. He wanted to do it all. He wanted to finger her, eat her out, and eventually get his enraged cock inside her and fuck her until "death" did him over or something like that.

As he kissed her he pushed himself against her body even harder as he tried letting her know how horny he really was. She knew but she loved how the young man kissed her so well.

"Mmmmm...ooohh" he'd hear her mutter off and on as her body seemed to squiggle left and right into his. As he went back down on her boobs and kissed and sucked them too she uttered and made him feel as though there wasn't anything better in the world. "Ohhh Jarrod...Jarrod...feel my...crotch baby... Oh feel me down...below honey" and as quickly as she said it his hand was inching its way inside her thighs. "Oh...oh god, yes baby yes."

Before she realized it, she was pushing her skirt down off her body. Whatever or however he was doing what he had done, she loved how it felt and his fingers were a melting pot of sorts. Inside her underwear and feeling the warm and wet layers of her pussy, she found she loved how he felt her cunt and clitoris.

"Go down on me…eat me…finger and eat me up baby" she told him so he did.

He fingered her madly. He fingered her deeply. She pushed herself into his fingers as his face, and mouth, went at her pussy. Mmmmm, she tasted good he thought. He kept at it eating it, tasting it, and fingering it too as her pelvis pushed back at his mouth endlessly.

"ARE…YOU READY… I WANT IT…I WANT YOU… FUCK ME…GO IN ME" she screamed so he ripped off his jeans and went at her, quickly. OH…FUCK…YES FUCK" she let out. "FUCK ME MORE…HARDER…OHHHHHH DON'T STOP" she let out, but he did stop and he lay on top of her looking down at her.

"You're sexy…did you know that?" he said with a smile.

She looked at him. "Thank you…and so are you, Jarrod." Her body needed more. She stared at him hungrily. Finally she said it. "Fuck me some more like you did… Make me cum again. I soooo want another orgasm honey… Please…oh please" she pleaded.

She stroked it, lovingly, and made him hard, again. Once he was hard, he plied himself atop her and he banged her, hard. He loved banging her like that. Her legs, they went wild coursing around and then atop his shoulders. Her hold on his frame got tighter. She pawed at him as he assisted in squeezing out another orgasm… All due to him…all due to his love of sex with this woman and others as well. He came and she came too. He lay over her and smelled her beauty, looking her in the eyes as he breathed hard on each other. She pulled him closer and began kissing his lips softly again.

"Wow…what was I going to have you do today?" she asked serendipitously.

"Uhhh…I think I did it…for you, didn't I?" Jarrod asked with a smile.

"Oh, uh that was…mmmmm" and she smiled "part of it, but I did have some other things too…but they can wait, but this…what we did… ooohh now we have to do this again. That's for sure sweetheart. Name a time…and place… I'll be ready. Will you?" she said.

He leaned in, nodded, and he kissed her on her lips. "Whoa…you bet your sexy body I will be" he replied. Within 15 minutes afterward they were at it again.

The Female Doctor

The female doctor sat in her chair, listening to the patient. He was explaining, or trying to at least, his problems with his girlfriend. She slowly got lost, in a sea of dreams, as she looked at him as he spoke.

Actually quite a good looking woman, she wore her hair short and primped it daily keeping it alive and beautiful as if she was 25 again. She was not. She was on her way to 45 but that didn't matter she had as tone a body as any at 30 could have. Proud of it, this was her sea of dreams.

He stands up and I look at him curiously. What is the man doing? Okay, I know it, and you do too. He's as handsome as they come, she told herself in the dream. But why is he standing up? Why is he looking at me like that? Is there something on me or wrong? I casually look down. Oh, maybe it's this blouse.

Maybe I should have buttoned it one more button. I guess I'm showing a little too much bosom…a little too much cleavage for that matter? Or even this, she thought…maybe it's the skirt. I know…I know, she told herself, I shouldn't have worn this one. She pressed her hands against it and pulled it "further" down her legs. Yes, okay…it's too short. I know…yes, I know…I'm showing way too much thigh.

The client or patient continued to talk as she daydreamed about him and her, sexually. He walks around the coffee table, smiling, and looking right into her eyes. "Oh, don't do that Terrance, as she calls him. Please sit down" she says in her dreams. But what she thinks is this- Ohhh, come here…come closer…take my hand…take me to my house…and make mad passionate love to me.

That's what she was thinking as he went on and on. She like many women around her found him very good looking, in the best of shape, and one hell of a conversationalist and with that she wanted to undo his zipper as well as her own clothes and get it on with him. She could feel herself already. Her pussy, tightening and reverberating…ready for an orgasm as his command.

"But Doc" he went on to say as she daydreamed sexually about him "what do you think?"

Her concentration about him and her was done. She'd lost that train of thought and brought back to reality. "Uh, pardon me?" she said. "I'm sorry…repeat that?"

He did and she listened and answered him as she studied his face. Ohhhhhhh wow, he should have a million girlfriends" she told herself.

She was falling for him even though he wasn't coming on to the good looking psychologist. God, I wish he'd lean forward and slip his hand up inside my…thighs. God, yes I do. Do it man…make me…hornier then I'm already getting. I want to…I want to feel your naked body against mine, she told herself. Take off your shirt. Let me see your chest. Oh god, stop this Sherry. You know better. You know you… should be…more responsible…then this.

He shrugged his shoulders. "So what's your opinion? What do you think Doc?"

"Huh, pardon me?" she said again. "Oh…" and she threw out some technical bullshit at him she knew he'd understand. "…so I'll see you again when then?" she said to him. "Oh and I've started something new" she lied. "I give all my clients a hug letting them all know I care about them" and with that bullshit stated, she took hold of his body, and pressed herself hard against his it for a good long minute. "See…now how does that feel?" she asked as she looked hard into his eyes.

He smiled a bigger then life smile telling her he could go for a few of those per day. Then he left as she watched him, and his ass, walk out. "Ohhhhhhhhhhh god…damn…I'd sure like to bed down with him" she said aloud after he was gone.

Before she knew it and since she didn't have another patient for an hour and a half, she sat on the couch he was on and her skirt slid up her legs. Sherry's eyes closed as she began to feel the warmth of her thighs on her fingertips. Rubbing them, lightly, it didn't take long at all for her hand to find its way inside her pantyhose and underwear.

Sherry began with her clitoris moving slowly and surely inside her pussy.

"Oh…ohhh… Ohhhhhhhhhhh" she let out as she slowly slipped down off the couch a little. She fingered herself harder. She fingered it more rapidly. She wanted him so much, she worked at getting him back, kind of. His body was naked. His cock was long. He swung it in front of her face as a teaser and finally she took hold of it, slipping it inside her mouth. She sucked on it and she licked it all over. Before she knew it, her dream had him cumming all over her face and upper body.

"Ding dong" the door bell rang. She shook her head. "Who is that?" she asked herself. "Nobody is due for 45 minutes." She, as quickly as she could, pulled herself together, but not realizing it did not do it very well. Her shirt was still buttoned as before. Her hair was pretty much the same. But her pantyhose, they were a mess, and she did not even realize it as she stood and answered the door.

He did, almost immediately, and wondered why her pantyhose were so "messed up" all of a sudden. He had looked down. He made a curious face. He looked back up at her and simply stated he left something in her office. She told him to come on inside and get it, of course, and again she watched his ass walk away from her. Ohhh that ass… If only he'd let me hold it in my bed…I'd hold it and squeeze it and-

"Doc is something bothering you this morning?" he asked.

"Oh uh no" she said.

"May I ask a question then?" he told her.

"Sure…yes…anything, I suppose" she replied.

"Umm why are…your pantyhose all messed up?" he asked.

"My umm…pantyhose?" and she looked down at her legs. Ohhh god…shit…nice job. "Oh, that happens with certain kinds of pantyhose I buy. I don't know why I buy them either" she said flushed as hell..

54

"Well, okay…" he smiled and went on to say "You're a lucky woman Doc…you have a great set of legs…you really, honestly do" and he winked at her with a smile. "Oh and I will say this…I do love those hugs you give patients."

"Really, you do?" she said with great emphasis.

"Yes…in fact, I'd take one…from you Doc…any time of the day…or night. See you later, okay?"

He left and she went back to her seat. She pulled her pantyhose back down and pounded out an orgasm. "Ohhhhhhhhhhh wow…wow was…" and she was breathing a little hard "was that good" she said with a smile as she licked her fingers off. "When is he coming again? Then maybe I can get him to cum too." She smiled, stood up, and properly fixed her pantyhose.

Angel

Gary lay back in the deep, deliciously hot, scented water and began to relax. The stresses of his days work slowly started to melt away from his taut, tanned body as his mind wandered.

Fee had greeted him at the door having carefully prepared the bathroom for his arrival home. Aromatic candles burned seductively on the marble surfaces, warm, fluffy towels draped invitingly over the rails and the mirrored walls reflected the steamy atmosphere. She had been wearing the black silk nightdress he had chosen for her last summer. It was very short with a deep revealing neckline that barely concealed her ample breasts, her nipples clearly visible as the silky material caressed them when she moved.

She had led him by the hand to the bathroom, helping him to shed his work clothes as they mounted the stairs. Once there she left him to soak in the luxurious, soothing bubbles for a while, returning minutes later and closing the door behind her. Fee smiled as she surveyed the delightful scene before her.

"Thank you Angel, this feels wonderful" Gary murmured lazily, sinking deeper into the steaming bathtub, "Just what I need after the day I've had today."

Fee knelt by the side of the tub, picked up the soap and began to slowly lather his broad chest as he talked, her small hands rubbing and soothing the tight muscles in his shoulders and neck.

Gary laid his head back and closed his eyes as her hands slid over his tired body. He felt the familiar stirrings in his groin as her hands caressed his flat belly, his dick twitching into life. Opening his eyes he caught a wicked smile on Fee's face as she too had noticed his obvious excitement.

"Oh dear," she sighed, grinning, "I think that needs some attention, don't you?" she laughed. She leaned over further to reach for his rapidly swelling member and her breast escaped from its silken confines exposing a rosy pink nipple.

Gary's wet hand reached out and cupped the breast gently, leaning forward to lick the hardening nipple. She groaned out loud as his tongue snaked around the rigid bud and soft lips pulled on it lightly. Fee's hand disappeared under the bubbles and began to massage his heavy balls as his swollen dick stuck up out of the water.

Suddenly she withdrew and quickly stood up, her face flushed and her eyes bright with mischief.

"Not here Sweetheart" she said, "I have plans for us tonight, when you're finished in here put on your robe and come to our room" she added winking sexily at him.

With this, she slipped out of the bathroom leaving Gary intrigued and aroused. He climbed out of the steaming tub and slipped on his warm robe wondering as he tied the belt what she had in store for him.

Leaving wet footprints behind him on the carpet he padded down the hallway to their bedroom.

The room was, like the bathroom, seductively lit by scented candles and was lovely and warm. He listened to the heavy, driving rain battering the windows behind the deep red curtains and felt a glow of comfort inside himself.

The large chunky pine bed dominated their bedroom and it was towards this he headed, allowing the robe to slip from his broad shoulders and fall to the floor. Easing himself on four large pillows he lay back and waited.

Minutes later he stirred from his sleep to feel his arms being raised. Quickly orientating himself he was aware that one wrist was tied securely to the chunky bedhead and that Fee was in the process of securing the other wrist with a fine silk scarf.

"Shhhhhhhhhhhhh, Sweetheart," she whispered, "I want you to just watch and feel"

In the candlelit bedroom she stood before him, the light flickering over her soft skin as she let the thin straps of the flimsy gown fall from her smooth shoulders revealing her taut, full breasts. The nipples were a dusky pink and stood proud and erect as her nightdress ceased its downward journey and rested seductively on the swell of her rounded hips.

God! The very sight of those wonderful breasts made him hard for her again. Her hands cupped them tenderly then slid to her hips and nudged the garment from its resting place leaving it puddle in a silken pool at her feet.

Her pussy lips were clearly visible between her tanned legs; she loved to keep herself smooth and completely shaven. She knew he loved it.

Climbing onto the bed beside him, her breasts swayed enticingly as she leaned over to kiss his lips. He longed to wrap his arms around her as she kissed him passionately, her tongue snaking its way into his mouth.

Gary's hard dick was throbbing as her hands stroked his face and neck. She kissed his chin and chest with tiny butterfly kisses, breathing heavily as she explored his body with her fingers and her lips. Fee paused and flicked her tongue over his sensitive nipples, taking one between her lips and sucking softly on it sending ripples of excitement through his captive body.

He could smell her wonderful woman scent and it was driving him crazy. Her small fingers were circling his stomach, agonisingly avoiding his stiff eager cock. Stroking the outside of his thighs she let her hair trail across his belly and groin, bathing his engorged dick with its softness.

She began to lick his taut stomach leaving shiny, wet trails as her fingers caressed the soft skin of his inner thighs.

"Christ" he breathed heavily "Untie me please Angel, I need to touch you"

Fee put her fingers to his lips and whispered "Shhh, Gary, just feel"

His whole body was tingling with lust, every nerve ending was alive and active as she stroked and caressed him tenderly. The bulging head of his swollen dick was slick with precum oozing from him and it glistened in the flickering light.

Her hand began to stroke and massage his heavy, tight balls and he groaned out loud. Fee lifted her head from his tummy and asked, "Would you like me to suck you Sweetheart?"

"Oh God, yes!" he exclaimed, his legs stretching out and his toes curling, "I would love you to suck it Angel" he whispered urgently.

Her wet, pink tongue flicked across the head of his throbbing dick, licking away the precum that was leaking from him. Her free hand grasped his solid shaft and started to wank him slowly.

As her wet lips enveloped him he could feel the warmth of her sweet mouth, his hips straining as he attempted to push deeper into her mouth. She sucked him with passion, massaging his aching balls, her lips sliding up and down his stiff rod engulfing as much as she could.

Gary was ready to explode when she stopped and backed away, leaving him highly aroused and helpless.

She knelt by his side and let her hand roam across her smooth, rounded breasts, pulling gently on her stiff nipples. Her other hand travelled downwards and stroked her flat belly, her eyes dancing. She opened her tanned legs a little giving him a perfect view of her bare pussy, the outer lips swollen with desire slightly parted to reveal the inner pink folds, wet with her passion. God he wanted her!

Her fingers began to slowly rub and stroke her soaking cunt, circling her stiff clitty and slipping between her velvety smooth lips. He could see her wetness coating her fingers as she caressed herself, her eyes closed and her head to one side as she softly moaned.

His rigid dick stood upright and he tried to wriggle free from his silken shackles to no avail.

Opening her eyes she could see he was more than ready for her as she was for him. She offered her soaking fingers to his eager lips and smiled as he eagerly licked them, tasting her musky sweetness and sucking her fingers greedily.

She straddled him, her smooth legs either side of his thighs and leaned forwards brushing his face with her erect nipples.

"Suck them Sweetheart," she ordered.

Gary lost no time at all; he gently pulled the hard nipples with his lips and began to suck hard. Fee gasped at the intense wave of pleasure she felt, her cunt pulsating and her heart beating loudly. She could feel the juices running from her twitching pussy and dribbling down her thighs as he sucked hard.

"I need to be inside you Angel," he almost begged.

Understanding his urgency she reached down between them and grasped his pulsating cock. It was still wet with her saliva as she rubbed it firmly against her swollen clitty and coated the bulbous head with her juices.

He felt her fierce heat envelop his dick as she slowly began to lower herself onto him. Her cunt clung to him tightly as inch by inch she impaled herself deliberately. She felt every ridge and every vein as her hungry pussy devoured the stiff cock that was stretching her so deliciously.

His wrists were still tied as she began to fuck him slowly, raising herself almost to the top of his huge throbbing dick then plunging it deep inside her making whimpering little animal noises as she rode him so well.

Her hips swayed and ground against him and he longed to just wrap his strong arms around her soft body, grasp her ass and drive himself deep into her very core.

"Fee untie me" he begged, "Please Angel, I need to hold you"

Leaning over, she quickly loosened his silken bonds allowing him to touch her for the first time. Sliding his hands over her hips he firmly grasped her ass and held her tight as he thrust deep into her. Their bodies bathed in perspiration was reflected in the candlelight, her lips parted and eyes closed as he fucked her deeply and passionately. He felt her hot pussy bathing his hard dick with her flowing love juices.

Her orgasm built quickly and without much warning, she began to pant rapidly, whimpering as she felt herself cumming hard in great spasmodic waves of pleasure, bucking and grinding her hips as she tried to get all of his magnificent cock completely inside her. The muscles in her soaking hot cunt were shuddering and rippling, gripping him tightly and milking his own intense orgasm from him.

His dick plunged deep and hard into her until, with a low guttural moan he began to shoot streams of cum deep inside her, filling her with his hot seed. He held her tightly against him, needing to feel himself deep inside her, pumping his creamy load as they fed and encouraged each others orgasms, pulsating rhythmically as they both came hard for what seemed an eternity.

He wrapped his big strong arms around the small quivering body and held her close, her warm soft breasts crushed against his broad chest. Finding her mouth, he kissed her deeply and tenderly.

"Thank you Angel" he whispered as she snuggled closer and closed her eyes, smiling.

Bound For Vegas

My lover and I had never been to Las Vegas together before. She'd never really been shy but for some reason she always viewed Vegas as somewhere she could really "let her hair down". It was someplace where it was okay for her to be wild when no place else was. I never questioned it; I just accepted it. As a result of her outlook there were always limits on what we could do at home or on other vacations. There were certainly things I wanted to try that I was sure she'd enjoy but she wouldn't even talk about them... except in Vegas.

I guess I should tell you about us. We're a white couple in our mid-40s. My lover is the mother of two, five feet three inches tall and properly curved. She's not fat but she's not skinny either. She's got curves where a woman should and her D-cup chest is always fun to play with.

I'm five feet ten inches and built decently. I'm no muscle-rock but I'm not soft, fat or sloppy either. I've got some body hair but nothing overwhelming. In the "manhood" department I've got about 6.5" of circumcised cock. My lover and I both keep our private areas either shaved or well trimmed. Neither of us likes to hunt through a jungle for what we want.

So, we found ourselves planning a trip to Las Vegas for a long weekend. She had told me a couple times that she was looking forward to the trip so she could let her hair down and I knew what she meant. She was looking forward to doing a few things she normally wouldn't -- or for whatever reason felt that she couldn't. I planned to take full advantage of that and began my own scheming without telling her what I was planning.

As a matter of preparation I purchased her two outfits from an online lingerie dealer along with two sets of shoes that had modest heels -- one was 3" and the other a little bit higher. I also purchased a few other items that I kept secret from her until the Friday night we were there and ready to play.

The evening had started out just perfectly. We'd spent the day walking shops and looking at the casinos on the strip. We'd had lunch at

Margaritaville and random drinks in the various casinos. We'd gambled here and there eventually walking away a couple hundred dollars up -- which more than covered the items I'd purchased to bring with us. Back in our room we relaxed some and showered to freshen up for dinner.

We ate at the Brazilian Steakhouse and it proved well worth what we spent. (Thank goodness for those gambling winnings!) After dinner we enjoyed another leisurely stroll back down the strip to our hotel where we spent probably another half hour or so in the casino. Between her winning at Blackjack and my luck in the slots we ended up another few hundred dollars ahead.

When she'd had enough gambling she asked me what I wanted to do next and that was when I told her that I had an adventure planned for her. With a careful smile and raised eyebrows she asked me what I had in mind. I told her that it was a sexy adventure and that I wouldn't tell her anymore about it. I told her that I needed her to just trust me, place herself and her well being in my hands, and enjoy the adventure. She asked how wild the adventure would be.

I refused to answer. "Trust me and jump blind or don't jump at all," I told her. "Don't make me dare you," I added on. I knew that would push her over the line. She can't stand the idea of turning down a dare; never has been.

"Okay," she said after a few minutes. "I'll bite. I'm yours o do with as you see fit. Take me on this adventure." I gave her a hug and led her to the elevator where we headed up to our room. Once there I asked her to strip down and she eagerly complied. Once she was naked I reached into my bag and pulled out the black silk blindfold. Her eyes opened wide when she saw that but she didn't say anything and she didn't back down.

As she stood still I put the blindfold on her and told her that she was not allowed to take it off until one of two things happened. She had to wear it until either I said the evening was over OR until such time as she decided she couldn't enjoy the adventure anymore and said the safe word. I told her that the safe-word was "cunt". It wasn't a word she would normally say so if it came out of her mouth I would know that

63

everything needed to come to a screeching halt. She told me she understood and asked what was going to be going on that I thought she might need a safe word. I refused to tell her, reminding her that she'd agreed to do whatever I wanted and to trust me that she'd enjoy herself. With that said and her blindfold in place I took out the outfit I wanted her to wear.

Although she couldn't see it I knew she'd feel it as she dressed so it wouldn't hurt to tell her what it was. "On the bed next to you," I told her, "there is a pair of pantyhose and a robe. On the floor next to the bed are the shoes you are to wear. If you need any help, just let me know."

I had to help her get the pantyhose in her hands properly so she'd know front from back and I guided her to the shoes. I held the robe for her and helped her adjust it before she tied the belt. The outfit was all black. The pantyhose were the kind that had no coverings for her ass or pussy. It was like stockings with built in suspenders and a garter belt but was all one piece made of the same sheer material. The robe was black silk, matching the blindfold and was long enough to cover her to about mid-thigh.

It was cut so that, tied shut, it crossed almost directly in the center of her cleavage leaving it obvious that she didn't have on a bra underneath. Thanks to the silk material, when her nipples hardened with excitement -- or from the caress of the silk -- it was obvious because they were making noticeable and easily seen bumps in the silk. Since she was wearing no panties or bra her curves moved easily beneath the material and she looked exquisite as she walked around the room for me.

Before moving on in the adventure I had her do exactly that. I pointed her in a direction where she wouldn't walk into anything and told her to walk until I told her to stop. Almost immediately she put her hands up to feel the air in front of her to make sure she wouldn't run into anything.

I explained that was unacceptable; that if she was going to trust me through the remainder of the evening and our adventure she'd have to trust me completely. I told her to put her hands down to her sides and walk until I told her to stop. She did as I asked and I told her to stop well before she'd have run into the sliding glass doors on the balcony. Then I had her turn and walk back to me which she did without hesitation.

Turning her around again I told her to stand still for a moment and I went to open the balcony doors. I know she heard me do it because when I told her to walk forward again she slowed down when she thought she was getting close to the doorway. I talked her through the next couple steps until she was on the balcony with me.

Our balcony was above the courtyard of the hotel and several other people were out on their balconies enjoying the evening as well. About half of them were men, but all of them seemed to turn and look at my lover. There she stood in her robe and hose, naked beneath and blindfolded so she couldn't see how many people may or may not be looking at her.

Stepping to her I put my arms around her and pulled her to me, grabbing in both my hands the cheeks of her delectable ass and kissing her passionately. I loved her so much. She was so trusting... and she was going to have SO much fun. She returned my kiss with equal passion until I pulled away and turned her back into the room.

Leading her by the hand I took her back over to the bed, reached in my bag and pulled out her last "garment". It was a circular length of rope about 18" long made of a soft cotton / silk blend. The key word there is SOFT as it was difficult to get a rope burn from it. Being circular it had been specifically designed as a voluntary retention device; a soft pair of handcuffs if you will that could be as tight or as loose as the wearer desired.

For my purposes it would be put on snug but my lover could release it anytime she wanted. I told her to put her hands out in front of her with her wrists almost touching and her palms facing each other. She complied. I looped the rope over her wrists, grabbed the dangling end and pulled it up in between her wrists and wrapped it around twice.

What resulted was essentially a pair of soft rope handcuffs, snugged by the rope wrapped around the middle. I put the dangling end in her right hand and told her to hold onto it. She complied. I explained the restraint to her and also explained that she was only restrained as long as she held onto the rope. If she let go she could easily unloop the rope and loosen / remove the "cuffs". She acknowledged her understanding and then surprised me by promising not to let go of the rope unless or until I told her to.

"Very good," I told her with a smile, noticing how excited she was as demonstrated by her perky nipples. "Now come with me," I continued, gently taking hold of her left arm and leading her to the hotel room door. She hesitated for a moment at the room door when she realized that I was taking her out into the hallway, obviously not sure she wanted to go out in public dressed as she was, blindfolded and "handcuffed".

As she stood there I reminded her that she could release herself anytime she wanted and had only to say a single word to end the adventure. OR, I emphasized, she could trust me and enjoy the adventure I had planned. With a deep breath she stepped out the door and allowed me to guide her to the right down the hallway toward the elevators.

From our room door the elevators were about a hundred feet down the hall. I walked the first twenty feet holding her by the arm but then I let go and told her she should keep walking. She paused only briefly but then held her head high and kept going. I slowed down so that I could watch her delicious ass swish beneath the black silk robe as she walked.

When we were about thirty feet from the elevators I heard the doors open and realized that someone was getting out. I looked carefully at my lover to see if she'd hesitate but she didn't let me down. I sped up so that I was right behind her and whispered to let her know I was there. She nodded quickly but didn't stop walking. We could both hear voices as whoever was in the elevator stepped out and approached the hallway intersection.

Their voices stopped mid-sentence when they saw my lover. They followed her with their eyes as she walked by and I gave them a wink when they looked at me as if to ask, "What's going on?"

A few feet farther down the hall I looked back and they were still standing there staring at her as she walked. Feeling a bit bold I reached out and flipped up my lover's robe, giving them an unhindered view of her framed ass wiggling as she walked. She felt the breeze and I saw her hips twitch but she didn't stop walking.

We went all the way to the end of the hallway to the stairs and I opened the door for her to lead her in and down. One flight down we walked back half the length of the hallway to the elevators. She knew where we were from the sound of the elevator chimes but she seemed perfectly at ease -- and still totally turned on.

I wondered how wet her pussy was but didn't dare reach under her robe to find out... yet. When the elevator doors opened there was an older couple standing there. Neither said a word as I led my restrained and blindfolded lover into the elevator, positioning her so that her back was to the man, her butt less than a foot from him covered in nothing but that silk robe.

I looked over at the panel and saw that they had pushed the lobby button. That was fine with me. No one said anything as we rode down in silence, but when we got to the lobby and the door dinged the man said, "Excuse me," and my lover about jumped out of her skin. Her first reaction was to step away from him but then she registered the casino floor noise and hesitated to move.

Any step she took would place her closer to the casino and I wasn't holding onto her at that moment. As soon as I touched her she seemed to relax a bit.

Taking her by the arm as the doors opened I led her out into the lobby. We walked a short circuit around the elevator area and the first couple of slot machine stands. Several men and women stopped playing so that they could watch my lover walk by.

I could hear my lover's breathing accelerate as she registered the fact that dressed in what little she had on, blindfolded and with her hands voluntarily tied, she was walking around in public. I knew that somewhere inside of her she was loving it. It was exciting her and she was reveling in how daring it was. Another part of her was scared and I made sure I maintained contact with her to keep that part comforted.

Back at the elevators I pushed the button and stood behind my lover, up against her so she could feel how hard I was, the bulge in my pants pressed up against her butt and lower back. Several other people joined us in waiting for the elevator and each of them tried not to stare. When the doors opened we all piled in and I positioned us so that my back was to a wall with my lover's ass backed up against me so she could continue to feel how hard I was.

As I looked down across her front I saw how perky her nipples were and I saw several of the guys in the group noticing. They saw me looking and I saw the looks of wonderment on their faces. I thought about reaching around her to cup her chest and give them a little bit of a show but I didn't want them to mistake it for an invitation so I settled for keeping my hands on her hips, slowly humping my hard cock against her silk robe covered rear end.

The elevator stopped at several floors with all but one of the people getting out before the floor I'd selected. I looked at the buttons and realized that the one remaining passenger was getting off one floor above ours. My lover had no idea how many people were left in the elevator with us. Neither he nor I spoke. As I saw him looking at her chest in the couple of floors left before our stop, I slowly pulled one side of her robe open, baring her nipple and breast to his view. I watched him look down at it in appreciation and then look back up at me, askance in his eyes. I shook my head no to let him know that he could only look -- nothing else.

I left her robe open and caressed her naked breast, cupping and lifting it, gently squeezing it, and milking my fingers down to softly pinch and pull her hard nipple. I heard her moan with the pleasure of it and then the floor bell dinged and the doors slid open. I started to close her robe but decided not to. I don't know why.

Holding her by the hips I shuffled her forward and out the doors, turning right down the hallway. When we got to the proper door I spoke to her quietly to give her some minor direction.

"Are you doing okay, baby?" I asked her quietly. She nodded a positive response. I was worried that she wasn't actually and was only nodding yes to make me happy. "Please give me a verbal response," I said to her. "Are you doing okay?"

"I'm fine," she said softly.

"Are you enjoying yourself so far?" I asked.

"I've been scared here and there," she said honestly, "but I've also been very excited."

"Do you trust me to make sure nothing bad or unwanted will happen to you?" I asked her.

"Absolutely," she said confidently.

"Then we're going to go into this room. Speak only if you're spoken directly to. Don't worry about what voices you hear around you or close to you. If anything happens that doesn't feel good, say your safe word. Do you understand?" I could see her trembling. I could see how erect her nipples were. I could see her thinking hard and wondering if she should overcome her nervousness. Ultimately she decided to trust me.

"Yes," she said in a quiet voice.

"Very well," I said to her seriously. "Then unless you are specifically asked something, you won't speak again until I say so or until you say your safe word." She nodded, I smiled and then I knocked on the door.

When the door was opened I led my lover in amongst appreciative eyes. The door closed behind us as I led her further into the room. On the television a porn movie was playing.

I glanced over and saw a scene where a brunette was on a bed on her back with a man kneeling on either side of her head; she was going back and forth between them, stroking and sucking the impressive hard cocks they were offering. Another man was between her legs stroking his even more impressive rock hard length in and out of her obviously very wet pussy. The noises escaping her were muffled by the fact her mouth was full of stiff manhood but it was still obvious she was having a good time.

Directing my lover by her hips still I walked her over to the sliding glass door that was open and walked her out onto the balcony. We both knew she was outside. Reaching around in front of her I untied her robe and slowly pulled both sides open to her hips.

Her beautiful chest, sexy hips and carefully trimmed sex were on display for anyone who cared to look up at that particular balcony at that moment. We were several floors up so they wouldn't be able to identify her and we weren't going to stand there long, but she had no way of knowing either of those things. For all she knew we were on the ground floor and anyone walking by could see her nakedness.

Leaving the robe open I turned her and walked / led her back into the room. On the television the brunette was now on her hands and knees being fucked hard doggy style while the other two men knelt in front of her and she alternated back and forth sucking them. Her moans and groans of pleasure may have been inspired by the paycheck she was receiving for the scene, but they added a tasty flavor to the atmosphere of the room.

I heard my lover's breathing pick up some and knew that her excitement was still growing. I knew she was very aware of her hands being restrained -- still at her own control -- and her nudity in front of a number of men (and women?) that she could only guess at. I was quite proud of her that she didn't say her safe word right then, releasing her hands at the same time and pulling her robe shut.

Leading her on two circuits of the room I let the eyes present get a good view of her body before I led her over to the bed and directed her to sit on it, then helping her to the middle and helping her to lie down. Once she was reclined on the bed, still naked, her legs pressed closely together and her nipples looking rock hard, I leaned over to her, kissed her gently on her cheek, and whispered, "I love you and am so proud of you," in her ear. I heard her sigh quietly as if those words were all the comfort she needed to calm herself and saw her body visibly relax a bit.

Taking hold of the soft robe binding her wrists I moved her hands up above her head to the headboard and hooked the rope onto the steel S-curve hook that was positioned there. I stretched her fingers out so she could feel what she was hooked to and the rubber bands that connected the S-curve to the headboard.

I wanted her to understand that if she wanted to she could get loose by pulling the rubber bands down and then disconnecting the S-curve either from the rubber bands or from her rope bindings. It was important to me that she understand that her continued restraint was entirely her own choice. She could escape it anytime.

I watched her carefully to make sure she understood before moving away from the headboard. Moving to the foot of the bed I caressed and then firmly gripped her right ankle, pulling it toward the corner of the foot of the bed and forcing her to spread her legs -- at least her right one that much. She resisted for a moment, tested the bonds at her wrist, and then -- apparently after reconfirming she could get loose if she wanted to -- she relaxed her leg enough to let me pull it over.

The bindings at the foot of the bed were NOT something she could simply pull her ankles out of or away from. The padded ankle-cuff was held by a leather strap to the foot of the bed frame. As I clicked the padded ankle-cuff into place around her right ankle I looked up the length of her leg to see her sex wetter than I'd ever seen in pre-sex before. With a smile on my face I moved over to her left ankle, pulled that leg over and attached the ankle cuff there too.

The Quickie Couple

I was on my knees cleaning out the bottom of my bathtub. Adorned in only cut off jean shorts and a bra. I was antsy and a bit nervous so I was trying to keep myself busy. You see my husband was due home tomorrow. He'd been away in prison for the past 3 years. I missed him so much but, I was worried about whether things would be awkward between us. Just then I heard a noise in the hall behind me. I look over my shoulder to find my husband standing behind me. He has just as nervous a look on his face as I do.

I didn't know exactly what to do so I turn on the shower water and asked him if he felt like taking a shower. "There are other things I can think of" he answered. I smiled a crooked smile and it dawned on me to ask as he approached me...."Why are...well I thought....How did you get here so early?" He did not answer as he grabbed me up into his arms and hugged me fiercely. I fumbled around trying to get comfortable in his arms. He let's me go and gently grabs my face. The kiss he gave me empowered me. I started to remember. Comfort started over me.

I needed him. My pussy started to get wet just looking at the hungry look in his eyes. I was worried that advancing on him might be too much too soon. I did not want to thrust my needs to heavily upon him. But after three years I needed him like he could never imagine. Trust me...I went thru a few vibrators while he was gone but they never put it to me like he could. Suddenly twisted out of my thoughts he moves closer to me and I feel HIS growing need.

He wraps his arms around me and pushes me back till my back was braced against the shower door. He smiled at me and ran his hand down my side till it was curved around my ass. Then he ran it down further to the back of my thigh, he lifted my leg up and my instinct was to wrap it around him yet he stopped me. He had me set my foot on top of the toilet lid. He then kissed my neck, then down to my nipples thru my bra, next my tummy. I started then to feel my pussy jump. I could feel his breath right outside the seat of my jeans.

Instead of putting his lips there, he started to smell me there. I looked down at him and he replied that it had been so long since he smelled the scent of a turned on woman he just wanted to remember. He pulled aside the crotch in my jeans and I felt his fingers slide into me I leaned back into the shower door and as my breathing got heavier I stopped myself from begging him to just take me.

Ahhhh I moaned. He started to go in and out of me with his fingers. My pussy dripping more and more. I can feel myself leaking my juices covering his hand. Soon enough his mouth followed. His tongue lapping over my clit. His non stop assault to my clit aided by the ever steady way he finger fucked me led me to my first explosion. I came so hard that when I was done I looked at his face I had squirted so hard there was cum still soaking his lips.

He stood up and took off all of his clothes right there. As his cock stood at full attention he reached for my shorts. He removed them and turn me around; he bent me over and slowly slid his cock into my waiting hole. I clenched my muscles around him as he entered me.

He buried his cock to the base inside of me and stilled for a moment. Soon he was building himself a rhythm, I hung onto the towel rack bar and took the pounding he administedered. After awhile I could feel myself starting to want to cum again.

I couldn't let that happen just yet. I reached back and pushed him away from me. When I faced him his dick was still at full mass and dripping my juices off the tip. The pre cum that leaked from his tip made my mouth water.

I got down onto my knees and approached him seductively. I wrapped my hand around him and drew him into me. I took first just the tip of his cock into my mouth. The taste of our juices mixed together was my undoing.

Inch by inch I took his entire tool into my mouth as I deep throated his cock I reached underneath and cupped his balls in my hand. I slowly and carefully fondled his balls as I picked up the pace of my deep throat. When his hand went to the back of my head I loosened up , and prepared for him to fuck my face. He pounded his cock into the back of my throat each time his balls slapped my chin.

He pulled his cock out of my mouth and slapped it on my cheek and tongue. He started to jerk his cock right in front of my face. I did not want him to waste his seed so I told him to lay down on his back. He laid there on the bathroom floor as I straddled him, and led his cock back to my pussy.

I got on top and slowly started to grind my hips on him. Back and forth I rocked riding him. Then I changed my motion and went with the up and down, I could see he appreciated the change and his body started to tense. I picked up the pace and just when he started to tell me he was going to cum I felt him let loose inside of me.

I jumped off of him just in time to catch a few squirts on my tongue and on my face. I took my finger to wipe off the cum on my face and sucked it off of my finger. I looked up at him to find him laying there smiling. Then he simply said...

"I missed you babe. Now how about that shower."

Barbra 's Confession

"Tell me the truth?" I asked my wife.

Barbra replied, " I'm nervous telling you what you have always suspected."

Her lovely green eyes averted my gaze as she continued, "I knew it was something that was going to happen. I would go in early when I knew only John was at work. The way I would present myself to him in those tight fitting outfits that you would allow me to wear."

She paused, adding, " It's difficult to tell you this."

With a slight grin, my cock getting incredibly hard visualizing her having sex with another man, I said to her, "Don't feel that way. You know I adore my perfect wife. Why don't you send me one of your stories that you like to write describing how you enjoyed yourself? I'd love to read it. But right now, I'm so incredibly turned on I'm going to take you to bed and fuck your sweet, willing pussy."

A couple of weeks passed and, as you could only imagine, I was unable to keep my hands off of her. Our sex life was truly amazing. Then one day, opening my e-mail at work early one morning, I received this letter from my loving wife:

" I always made it a point to get to the office before everyone else knowing that my boss was going to be there. I would sit in the car for a few moments before going in and would fuss over my hair and makeup in the rear-view mirror making sure it was just perfect. I would adjust my large breasts in those tight blouses that you like to buy for me and enjoyed John's glares when I came into the office.

I would walk through the door hoping for a look from him. Sometimes, I would remove the modesty button from my blouse and intentionally leaned over so that he could have a clear look at my tits. One morning, I found John in my office looking for a report I worked on the day before. Approaching him, he told me how stunning I looked. I was wearing that provocative low cut white blouse and tight black shirt that I always wear when you want to show me off. He explored my body with his eyes a moment longer than usual and I thanked him for the compliment. He asked me to sit at my desk and help with the report. When I sat down he leaned over the chair and put his hand on my shoulder.

My nipples began to get harder. He asked a couple of mundane questions about the report and began to slowly move his hand from my shoulder down towards my breasts. I turned toward him offering no resistance allowing him my tits.

I slipped my blouse over and unclasped my bra exposing myself and relished the idea of his hands on me. I was finally getting what I wanted for so long. John began caressing my tits circling my hard nipples with his fingers. I was eye to eye with his crotch and saw the bulge in his pants. My pussy was becoming very moist.

I stared at the outline of his growing cock. He brought his head down and began to suck on my nipples. I moaned with desire and pulled his face onto my soft breasts as he used his mouth on me kissing and biting my erect nipples. With my other hand, I reached over and started to squeeze his dick.

I felt the light touch of his tongue on me while I groped at his hard cock through his pants. Through the fabric of his trousers I could tell his cock was very thick. I tried to unzip his pants but he stepped back and pulled me up off the chair. He lifted up my skirt and then tugged at my red thong.

"Take off your panties," he demanded.

Reacting too slowly for him, he repeated himself in a sterner voice, "Barbra , do it now."

I pulled up my skirt and removed my panties. He grinned at my obedience. Looking into my eyes, he moved his hand down to my hot pussy. I let out a little sigh that was a mixture of apprehension and delight. He started to caress the folds of my pussy. I was incredibly turned on as his strange fingers explored me. I easily forgot all my promises and thought only of my desire to have his strange hands on me.

I pleaded, "Yes, John, that's it. Keep touching me. Oh, that feels so good."

He told me, "Barbra , spread your legs wider. Let me enjoy your gift to me."

I gladly opened up my legs for him. His breathing became deeper as he continued to feel his way around my swollen pussy. My juices were dripping down my thighs and he began to roughly finger fuck me. I felt as if I was going to cum right then.

I sighed, " Oh, yes sir, I love your fingers inside me. Keep going. Touch my clit. "

I held my breath when he put a couple of his fingers deep inside me while forcefully rubbing my excited clit with his thumb. I began moving my hips responding to the way he toyed with my pussy. I could feel his lust as he discovered me.

Then, crouching down with his fingers still fondling my pussy, he lifted up my shirt with his other hand. He hesitated for a moment to enjoy the sight of his prize. He fell to his knees and gently began to lick the folds of my swollen, wet lips. I remember holding onto his head balancing myself while he used his tongue on me.

He guided me back down into my chair.

With my skirt hiked up, I leaned back spreading my legs and wrapped my ankles around his shoulders allowing him full access to my hot pussy. He started to finger me again while he sucked on my inflamed clit. I squirmed around in the chair and moaned loudly as my boss continued to nibble on me.

I cried, " Oh, yes. Yes. Use your mouth on me. I love it. Yes, sir. Don't stop. Oh, yes. I want you to eat my pussy. Make me feel new again. Thank you John, thank you."

He spread my lips with his fingers and licked and sucked on my drenched pussy. I pulled his hair as I pushed myself into his face. I still get hot remembering the way he attacked my cunt and the slurping sounds he made eating me out.

When he realized that I was about to cum he stopped and forced my legs off his shoulders and stood up. I was sitting in my chair and spread my legs far apart. He brought his moist fingers to my mouth and with no hesitation I started to suck on them.

I could taste myself and John's eyes grew larger watching me suck on his fingers. I reached for him and unfastened his pants and pulled them down to his ankles. My eyes opened wide when I saw the size of his enormous stiff cock. It was about as long as yours but I was startled by his impressive girth.

His twitching cock was directly in front of my face and he asked me, "Barbra , do you want to suck my dick?" I replied, recalling a past vow, "Yes, I do."

I grabbed his thick cock with my hand and began to lick the pre-cum off the head of his dick. I slowly licked him from his balls along the underside of his cock flicking my tongue on the soft and sensitive underside of the head of his dick. I rubbed his fat, hard meat over my face. I was kissing and licking and scratching his dick with my manicured bright red nails.

Standing above me, while I used both my hands to explore his thick dick, John said, "That's a good girl. I knew you loved dick. I'm sure you feel special making a man hard. You're very talented. I want you to play with my hard cock."

I whispered, as I patted my lips with his manhood, "Yes, sir. I am very proud of myself."

He grabbed the back of my hair and I needed to open my mouth more than I was use to when I began to suck on his cock. I tried getting use to his girth and was moving cautiously going down on his cock when he pushed my mouth further onto his dick.

He told me, "That's it, I want you to take all of it," He kept up the pressure on me by pushing down on the back my head down with his hands. I couldn't breath and tried to pull away from him. My eyes watered and I began to gag with his huge cock so deep down my throat.

With what little mercy he would show me, he finally released his grip on my hair. It took a moment for me to regain my composure. I wanted desperately to impress him and with a renewed purpose I went down his rock-hard cock until I was finally able to take all of him. Even though unable to control the tears in my eyes I wrapped my lips around the base of his shaft. I started to suck harder on him and went up and down on his meat.

My blouse was open and the front snaps of that sheer bra you love so much was unclasped showing off my large excited nipples. I felt important with my legs open and my pussy was quivering from all this attention my boss was giving me. He sighed with pleasure as I enthusiastically sucked on his dick. I was moaning while I was giving him this blow job letting him know how much I loved going down on him. I was getting very hot and my cunt was beginning to ache for more attention. As I sucked on his big dick, I was imagining how it would feel slamming into my needy pussy.

Just then he started to pull out of my mouth. I tried to stop it and sucked even harder on him but he withdrew and the sounds of my lips smacking together resonated through the office. I lunged forward opening my lips trying to get his dick back into my mouth but he held me back with one hand and started to masturbate with other. He was only inches from my face and I watched him jerking off as I felt the tenderness in my jaw from sucking on such a thick cock.

His pace quickened and he started to cum and then exploded all over my face. He let out such a burst of cum that it splattered all over my face and dripped down past my chin and onto my blouse. I fingered some of his warm spunk back into my mouth and smiled to him as I licked his juice off my lips.

Catching his breath, with his cum all over my face, he told me, "Barbra , you look perfect. I can only imagine what it's going to be like when I fuck you."

I said to him, " I can't wait to have your dick deep inside me. Fuck me like I want to be fucked. I need for you to spread my dirty twat open with your big cock."

He then grabbed me by the arms and lifted me on my desk with my paperwork flying off the desk onto the floor. He forcefully spread open my thighs. I was flattered he was able to get hard so quickly again. I was incredibly excited to finally get my wish and have him plunge into my pink-swollen pussy. I could feel my juices dripping down towards my ass.

He grabbed onto his hard dick and thrust it into my eager pussy. He took my ankles and spread my legs even more. I could see my rose tattoo on my ankle while he held my feet high in the air. He picked up the pace and fucked me harder. I felt very defenseless lying on my back while John was giving me this punishing fuck. I began to cry out as he drove in and out of my swollen pussy. I was moaning with pleasure taking his massive tool deep inside me.

He lifted up my legs and tightened his grasp on my ankles as he grinded inside me. I could tell he was enjoying the sight of fucking me while he explored the recesses of my pussy with his cock. My large breasts were bouncing up and down every time he plowed into me. My legs were becoming sore spread so wide open and being held so high up.

His dick was unbelievably hard. I moved my hips rhythmically to meet his cock. He was pounding harder and deeper into me with every thrust.

I screamed, "That's it. Yes. Oh, yes. Please John, fuck my cunt with your superb cock. Push it deeper inside me. Use it. That's right. That's how I need to be fucked. Fuck me just like this. I love it."

My pussy was so alive that when I met him with my clit I felt a wonderful tingling sensation. I began to feel flush and tensed up and let out a long, loud cry as I came, tightening my raw pussy around his dick. My head moved back and I closed my eyes, panting with satisfaction in total ecstasy. Seeing the look on my face excited him. With one final thrust, and I honestly thought he was going to tear me open, he spurted into me and gave his new slut some more cum. I smiled in satisfaction feeling his cock pulsating inside me after he deposited his juices in my used pussy.

Realizing the time, I got dressed in a rush. I could only manage to put the red thongs into my purse. I quickly put all the scattered paperwork back on my desk. John gave me a tender peck on the cheek as he walked towards his office. I happily recalled the way he pushed my legs wide open to accept his cock.

I momentarily lost track of time.

I remembered the way he grabbed onto my ankles and filled me up. I could still feel his cum dripping down my legs as I tried to concentrate on getting back to work. I began to wonder if this was going to become a morning routine with him. Needing to clean up before the others arrived for work I went to the bathroom. Looking in the mirror, I saw his cum all over my face and neck.

I quickly got a paper towel and washed my face. There was so much there. I could hardly believe that anyone could cum that much. Looking in the mirror only confirmed what a willing little slut I was for my boss.

Going into his office later that day he would once again reach inside my stained blouse and play with my tits. I could only smile as he caressed my tits and then moan as he reached up my skirt as I willingly spread my legs while he fondled my bruised pussy.

Later, leaving work, I reached into my purse and noticed my red thong that I placed away earlier and wondered what will happen tomorrow?

Lisa and Nick

I was away for two weeks on business. My wife and I tried to phone each other every night but a couple of times she explained that she couldn't talk and needed to work late. Lisa always called the following morning telling me how she missed me and wanted me home.

'I miss you too. I constantly daydream about you," I would tell her.

I could see her smiling as she asked, " What do you dream about or do I already know?"

I thought about her last e-mail, admitting how she loved sucking his dick and the hard fucking her boss gave her one morning before work. My cock was getting hard fantasizing about her taking off her clothes and getting fucked by another man.

I told her, " I always dream about my beautiful wife. Why don't you send me one of your stories to help me pass these lonely nights while I'm away?"

She replied, "I've been working hard on one since you left. I'll send it to you tomorrow."

The next day she called and told me she was tied up at work and couldn't get away. I was disappointed and then she told me, " I just sent you something for your last night away. Let me know if you like it?"

I hung up the phone and, with my heart racing, turned on my computer. I opened my e-mail and found her message:

"The following morning, I took a hot cleansing shower. I paid particular attention to my used pussy, shaving it clean and leaving only a thin strip on top. I masturbated in the shower remembering how my boss grabbed my ankles spreading my legs apart and pounded his thick cock into me. I fantasized about sucking his dick and my face being splattered with his hot cum. I came hard thinking of what a dirty, little submissive I was for him. I took some extra time applying my make up and decided to put on my brightest red lipstick.

82

I was impatient driving to work. I posed at the door to his office wearing a sheer blouse and my shortest shirt that you laid out for me on the bed and my black high heels. I also put on my black thigh-high stockings, which revealed the lace tops when I sat down. Anyone who saw me understood my intentions. Nick turned around in his chair admiring my body and said, "Lisa, you look absolutely sensational. I was very anxious to come to work today."

I responded with a big smile.

He told me, "Lisa, come over here."

I walked over to him. His pants were unzipped and his big cock was standing straight up. I was extremely proud of myself that I could make a man so hard so quickly. I smiled to myself as I gawked at his hard cock. I knew it was just for me. I licked the palm of my hand and reached down and ran my hand over his dick. I could feel the heat of his meat as I fondled and stroked him.

He reached up my skirt and ran his fingers over my stockings and caressed my thighs before he delighted himself by groping at my soft pussy. I cupped his balls in my hand and leaned over and spit on his cock the way certain girls know how to do so that my hand could slide easier up and down his cock. He was caressing my ass and tugging at my thong while I was giving him a proper hand job.

I could feel his raging hard on becoming as hard as a piece of steel and knew he was only moments away from cumming when he seized my wrist and stopped me. "Lisa," he said, looking intently into my eyes and sitting back in his chair, " I want you to take off your blouse and bra for me."

I was staring at his throbbing cock and I was very excited to undress for him. I could feel my nipples becoming harder as I slowly unbuttoned my blouse and removed my lace bra. I carelessly let the expensive clothes you bought me fall to the floor as I undressed for him. He leered at the sight of my large perky milky white breasts. His gaze washed over my body. Waiting for his instruction, I stood perfectly still wearing only my skirt, stockings and high heels.

Nick stood and his stiff dick pointed at me as he approached me. He ran his fingers through my hair and began to nibble at my neck. He started to roughly fondle my tits and I moaned as I arched my back enjoying his hands on me. He bent down and kissed and sucked on my hard nipples. I reached for him and closed my eyes as I clinched onto his cock.

I spread my legs for him as he ran his hands over my thighs. Every time he bit my nipples I squeezed his cock even harder. I was getting incredibly turned on with the way he was man handling me. He moved behind me and I kept holding onto him. I could tell he was taking his tie off. All of a sudden I felt him reaching for my hands forcing me to release my grip on him. He took the tie and strapped my wrists together. My heart was pounding.

I could feel his breath on the back of my neck when he whispered into my ear, "Lisa, I want you to get on your knees."

With no reservation, I fell to my knees. With my hands tied behind my back, I was forced to accept that I was his perfect submissive and understood I could be used how and when he wanted. He stepped in front of me. I was staring at his dick while he reached into his back pocket and brought out a blindfold. The last thing I saw before the blindfold turned the room dark was his rock hard cock only inches from my face.

I was amazed that I could feel so vulnerable and content at the same time. I knew the blindfold was a sharp contrast to my milky complexion and red hair. He told me, " I want you to stick out your tongue."

I licked my lips and showed him my tongue. He grabbed my hair and directed my mouth down onto his balls. I began to lick him. I felt the warm fuzziness of his firm balls as I tongued and then sucked them into my mouth. I occasionally felt his fingers as he played with his dick. He clinched onto my hair forcing my head back and began to rub his cock around my lips. I could taste the pre-cum dripping from his cock and could feel the trails of his cum while he moved his magnificent cock all over my face. My pussy was dripping wet.

I heard him order me, "Lisa, open your mouth."

Opening my mouth for him he used his dick to toy with me and slapped my lips and then slapped my face with his heavy dick.

" Take all of it in your mouth. Give me one of your wonderful blow jobs," He said.

In one motion, I went down on him and took all of him into my mouth. With his meat buried in my throat I imagined leaving a bright red mark around the base of his cock from my lipstick.

He forced my head up and down on his cock and fucked my mouth for several minutes. I was amazed at his stamina and was very disappointed that I couldn't make him cum. I continued to suck on him until he placed his hand on my chin and then pushed me away.

Wanting more, I cried, " Please Nick, give it back to me." But my pleas were dismissed.

My lips were still moist from the blow job I just gave him. I could feel the juices from my quivering pussy beginning to surge. I started to speak but he told me to remain quiet. Suddenly, he reached around and grabbed my bound hands.

He stood me up and turned me around and then untied my hands. Waiting for his next demand, I must have been quite a sight standing there blindfolded and topless with my lips still glistening from sucking his dick.

I heard him rummage through his desk.

"Nick," I started to ask what he was getting out his desk drawer but he cut me off.

"Don't worry, you'll have fun. We'll all enjoy ourselves," he told me.

Questions and scenarios raced through my mind. What did he have? What was going to happen? What did he mean, "we'll all enjoy ourselves?" I was nervous and incredibly excited at the same time.

He said," Lisa, take a couple of steps back. Let me look at you."

I cautiously stepped back. Seconds passed, but it seemed like an eternity.

Finally, Nick spoke to me, "You look stunning standing there with the blindfold on and wearing that sexy skirt and heels. I want to watch you play with your tits and those excited, beautiful nipples for me."

I reached up and began to touch my breasts. Being on display, I slowly used my fingertips to softly caress my tits. I teased myself and ran circles around my erect nipples with my fingers before I playfully pinched them. I threw my head back cupping my breasts in my hands. I let out a soft moan as I roughly fondled my large tits.

He said, "My dick is straining watching your lovely red nails playing with yourself. I want you to suck on your fingers."

I could only imagine his satisfaction watching me suck on my fingers as I pinched and twisted my hard nipples. My thong was soaked putting on this show for him.

Suddenly, I heard a familiar sound. What was it? I was shocked when I realized it was the noise of a photo being taken. I stopped playing with myself.

My boss raised his voice, " Lisa, keep doing what I told you to do." He added, almost imperceptibly, "Besides, your husband asked for some pictures of his wife working."

My heart was beating so hard the silence in the room was almost deafening. I wondered when you talked to Nick? Then I remembered. I arrived late one night at a bar found you and Nick sitting in a corner booth. The conversation abruptly ended as I approached you. Blindfolded, and on display, I can see clearly now the furtive glances you exchanged when I sat down. You explained that you were having a very pleasant discussion but admitted the conversation was mostly about me. Nick's smirk at the table now tells me you talked about me in a submissive role with another man. I was vulnerable and remembering the conversation at the bar, I became flush and my knees started to weaken. Nick recognized this and said, " Lisa, you shouldn't feel like that. He knows how much you want sex. How you adore having the sexual control over a man by teasing him. The way you use your body and your words letting him know how available you are. How the attention thrills you and the confidence you have knowing you can make any dick hard any time you want." He paused and added, " And the way you so easily spread your legs inviting a man's dominance over you."

He came closer and forced me to bend over the soft leather chair. I tried to speak but all that happened was an ignored soft plea. He came behind me and lifted up my skirt. With a firm smack he hit my ass with a ruler he must have taken from the desk drawer. I'm sure it left a thin red mark on my ass that I would be unable to hide from you. I was shocked and completely unnerved by this. I squirmed and tried to get up but Nick used his hand to hold me down. I was unable to move and had absolutely no protection.

Finally, he demanded, "Tell me what a slut you are."

My body was shaking and between breaths I was only able to let out a soft whimper. Smack! He hit me on her other side of my ass. The second smack didn't seem to hurt as much; rather, it was more of a sting.

"Answer me," he voice was heightened.

"I'm a little slut," I said reluctantly.

"What kind of slut are you?" he asked, as he laid down a much harder smack on my firm ass.

Restrained and bending over the chair, I cried, "I'm a happily married slut who lets her boss fuck her. Please Nick, punish me with your thick dick. Stick it in me. Please, please, fuck my naughty cunt."

"That's a good girl," he said, as he gently began to rub my sore ass. My ass stung, but I was getting incredibly turned on by this.

He said, "I want to watch you masturbate."

87

My pussy was so hot I immediately moved my hand down between my legs. I pulled my lace black thongs down to my knees and began to play with my big wet folds. I could only imagine how he admired the control he had over me.

I sighed and my pussy was on fire and sopping wet. I moved my hips back and forth while I fingered myself. I heard the camera click a couple of more times. I heard him say, " My cock is rock hard and I can barely take another moment of watching such a horny slut playing with herself."

Saying that to me took me over the top and I felt as if I was going to cum but he stepped behind me and gave me a sharp slap on my ass and demanded, "Lisa, you are not allowed to cum just yet." It took what little self-control I had left to stop my orgasm.

I sensed him positioning himself behind me as he gave my delicate ass another quick squeeze. I could feel him at my cunt. Spreading my legs apart he selfishly shoved his big cock deep inside me. Plunging deep into my pussy he continued giving my ass more spankings as he moved in and out of me.

I was feverously rubbing my excited clit and cried out, "Yes. Fuck me. Please fuck me. I love your strong cock. Keep slapping my naughty ass. I deserve to be spanked. Push it in deeper. Pump it into me." "Tell me again how much you love my cock inside you", he demanded as he continued to give me a deep hard fuck.

"I love your big dick inside me. Give me more," I boasted.

Completely at his mercy, I challenged him and demanded, "Is that all you got? Fuck me harder. Make me cum. Pound your big cock deeper into my dirty cunt"

Nick redoubled his efforts with each thrust he went in deeper than the last. I thought I was going to pass out. He was grabbing my hips with both hands pulling me towards him as he drove his magnificent cock into my raw pussy. I was moaning loudly and started to tingle all over and felt like I was going to cum.

He knew this and said, "Don't make me tell you again -- don't cum you sexy whore until I tell you to." He gave me another firm slap to remind me who was in control. I moved my hand away from my swollen clit and was unable to do anything but take the brutal fucking he was giving me.

He was pounding into me and the room echoed with sound of him slapping against my tender ass. I could feel his cock getting harder and knew that his cum was building up inside of him. Grinding inside me, he caught his breath and said, "Lisa, you may allow yourself to cum now. It was only seconds later that I gave out a huge squeal and came as my boss gave me one more deep thrust and dumped his heavy load into my tender pussy.

Weekend In Nashville

About a year ago my wife was invited to visit Nashville for the weekend to make a presentation to an entertainment group and she invited me along for the ride. Since it had been a couple of months since we had had the opportunity for some time alone, I jumped at the chance for a weekend getaway with her.

We are a very sexually active couple who have been married for 23 years and make the most of two and three day weekends away. Not to miss the chance for this to be one of those, I charged up the video camera battery, picked out some nice toys and loaded the car for our trip south. After a nice drive into the Music City we checked into the Opryland Hotel and made our way to a beautiful room that overlooked one of the many gardens in the facility.

After unpacking and visiting one of the restaurants for dinner and a bar for a couple of drinks we decided to return to the room for some fun and excitement. The entire evening had so far been one of anticipation from both of us of what the rest of the evening would bring.

Once back in the room, my lovely wife retired to the tub for a hot, relaxing bath while I got the room ready for us. Once she was in the tub, I set up the video camera on a tripod in a position that would cover the entire bed and set the zoom lens for just the right level to capture everything. Then I ran some warm water in a bowl and got the razor and shaving cream ready (she really likes for me to shave her pussy completely bare on these trips) and dimmed the lights.

Once out of the tub, she emerged from the bathroom wearing a naughty but nice little red teddy that amplified the beauty of her 38 inch breasts. These breasts are magnificent with beautiful nipples that harden like rocks as she gets excited. Once she saw the camera and toys, her nipples began to harden and I knew that she was ready for anything. I set the camera to record as she settled into the king-size bed and began tweaking her already hard nipples.

As I knelt between her legs and spread the shaving cream on the lips of her now steaming pussy the juices were already flowing and I proceeded to slowly and carefully shave her smooth. I had already touched up my balls and pubic area so that it was smooth as silk also. There's just something highly erotic about two shaved pubic areas rubbing together that turns me on. Anyway, after finishing her up I moved up so that I could taste that hot musky area between her legs proceeded to lick and suck her pussy lips until she screamed with an incredible orgasm.

After coming back down from this beautiful experience, she pushed me onto my back and proceeded to suck my rock hard dick like there was no tomorrow. She started by circling the head with her tongue while stroking the shaft with her hand until she could take all 7" into her throat and began to slide her mouth up and down the shaft until I was ready to explode.

Let me just say at this point, that she is one of the best cocksucker ever. Her favorite position is to lay on her back while I kneel above her and after rubbing my dick over her nipples, she takes the shaft in hand and strokes it while sucking the head like a lollipop until I blow my wad all over her breasts.

By now her pussy was dripping with her hot juices and ready for some serious fucking. At this point I moved behind her and slipped the head of my dick just inside her hot pussy and then eased into her until the entire shaft was buried in her from behind and began to pump so that each time I drove in, my balls slapped her on the bottom and made her scream and beg for it to not stop.

After about 15 minutes of intense pounding from behind we changed positions to the missionary and she spread her legs wide for me to slam into her again and I continued this until we both climaxed with an incredible mutual orgasm and I filled her with my hot seed.

All of this was caught on tape and now we like to enjoy it at home together, many times with her on her back while I shave her sweet pussy.

As our 23 years together continues, our sex life is more incredible now than ever before. Our schedules have required us to spend much time, sometimes a week at a time, apart but our lovemaking time together is so intense that I want it to go on forever.

To my lovely wife, I love you and I'm headed to bed to join you now.

Jill and the Ball Player

My Name is Jill, I am a what some call an MILF. I'm 32 I have blonde hair, and a really tight body. I have size 34D boobs and an ass you could bounce a quarter off of. I have three kids all boys ages 14, 12, 9. My husband works long hours and I am normally the one to run the kids everywhere, being I'm a house wife. I have a story to tell about something I'm not proud of but I can't say I regret.

My boys are big baseball fans, we went to a pro baseball game. My son's are big fans of the local team. We went to the game and I found it quite boring except for the right fielder Rico Huerta who was a superstar player.

He had a great body and was very sexy. I was becoming quite the fan. My boys like to stay after the game and see about getting autographs. This time I was more than willing hoping to get a glimpse of Rico. Sure enough there he was, he shot me a smile and I shot one back. He came over and talked to the boys and I gazed at his beautiful body. He asked the boys if I was there older sister and they laughed as then told him that I was their mom.

He took pictures with the boys and was a great guy. He asked me over to take a picture, I went over and put my hand on his chest which was hard as a rock. He put his arm around me and put his huge hand on my ass. I was shocked but excited, whispered to me that he was staying at the local hotel and was in room suite 8. I was caught off guard and told him I was married, he said well its up to you.

I then piled the boys back in the mini van and headed home. The whole ride home all I could thing about was Rico and that rock hard body with those huge biceps. It had been a long time since my husband had touched me. I was so wet, my mind kept thinking about having that gorgeous man close to me and him putting his cock in my soaking wet pussy. He had been in all the papers dating all the hot celebs, he must be a great lover.

I made the boys dinner and told the oldest son that I was going out to meet their aunt and he was in charge. After putting the boys to bed. I got all dressed up, putting on my sexiest cocktail it is gold very short and with a neck that dips down to my bell button. I bought it on a whim and now have a reason to where it. I put on my sexiest black g-string and my perky tits bounced a little as I walked. My strong legs on display for everyone to see. I was going to do this and do it right.

As I arrived at the hotel it was crawling with ball players, I sat at the bar in the lobby and was hit on multiple times but I told them I was meeting my husband. I had a few drinks building up the courage to go give myself to a man that wasn't my husband. After about three drinks I was feeling ready and my pussy dripping wet from all the excitement.

I took the elevator up to suite #8. I knocked the door after fixing my boobs. He opened the door and he was there in just a towel as he had just jumped out of the shower. He was very happy to see me. He said he was glad I could make it and invited me in. He was so sexy, he had the perfect chest and I couldn't wait to see what was under the that towel.

We had a glass of champagne and went out to the balcony; you could see the entire city. He then toasted me for coming and he told me how beautiful I was. I stepped closer to him and we kissed. I could feel his cock growing under his towel as we continued to kiss. He then grabbed me and started to rub my ass. He brought his hands to my breasts and took them out of my dress. He gently kissed them and then he took my dress off my shoulders and it quickly hit the ground. I undid his towel and saw his beautiful cock.

He was 6 inches long and not completely hard, his cock had nice girth to it, almost as big as my wrist. I stroked it and and licked his balls. I then took his massive tool in my mouth, I was so hot for Rico. I played with his cock and it grew in my mouth, he was nowhere near coming. I then stood up and he took down my g-string. I leaned over the balcony and spread my legs giving him access to my wet pussy, he got behind me and placed his large cock in my pussy.

He slowly worked it in and before I knew it I was coming and screaming off the balcony. He was a machine pounding at my pussy, he just went faster and faster. I had orgasm after orgasm, I lost track of how many I had. He was slapping my ass with one hand and pinching my nipple with the other. He pounded my pussy for what had to be 20 minutes and then I felt him tense up and he let out a scream as his shot his load in my pussy.

We then laid out on the balcony still naked drinking champagne off each other's body and holding each other. I would poor the champagne on his cock and lick it off. After doing that a time or two his cock came back to life. I played with and sucked his cock some more. He he then picked me up and took me to the bedroom where he laid me on my back and I spread my legs open to expose my hungry pussy.

He then got on top of me and used the footboard on the bed for leverage and pushed deep in my pussy. I came again and again. He then grabbed me in his humongous arms and flipped me and had me ride his cock I let out scream after scream with each orgasm. I rode him for some time and then we both came at the same time. It was intense orgasm I had ever had.

I left back for home at about 4am after another go at it in the shower. I found the boys asleep when I got home. All I could think about in bed was how exhausted I was from the best night of fucking I had every had and ever will have. He gave me his number but I don't want to make a habit out of cheating on my husband he has a lot of girls wanting in on the action, but you never know.

My Wife The Tease

I'm a very lucky man! I have a beautiful young wife who I love very much. She is a petite 24 year old hottie who turns heads wherever she goes. She stands only 5" 2" tall and weighs only 105 pounds, but it's all in the right places, presenting a very curvy figure. Her tight little buns packed in a pair of jeans are something to behold, and she fills out a sweater quite well. To top it off her light brown hair, highlighted with blond streaks, is bobbed to the shoulders, curled under and to the front to frame an innocent face with a wide inviting smile; all giving her a pixie look. She works as a bank teller and is so cute that strange guys have actually approached her at her window, rose in hand, to ask her out. I have learned to live with the attention she gets and I must admit it makes me both proud and excited.

I must be reading too much porno and became obsessed with the thought of sharing her with another guy. I'm not sure why, but the thought of watching her perform for a stranger just drove me crazy! Part of it was letting someone know what I get all the time. . . . like showing off, I guess.

I fantasized about it when we had sex and began to include her in the role playing. The playing was fun for both of us and she seemed to get off on it, but would have nothing to do with the idea of doing it for real. But I kept pestering her about it and she kept refusing. Then one day she came home from the health club obviously excited and told me that we needed to talk. When I questioned her about it she said that it would have to wait until later when she could have a couple of drinks to loosen her up. Of course I was intrigued at that point and anxiously awaited our talk.

After dinner we sat together of the sofa, had a couple of glasses of wine and shared a joint. We were very mellow when she began.

"Michael, ya know the fantasy that we have been sharing recently?"

"Well, this new personal trainer just started at the club..."

You didn't fuck some guys this afternoon, did you?" I interrupted.

"Oh no," she reassured me, "He just showed a lot of interest in me, and I think he is hot."

"Oh, ya do, do ya?" I teased, feeling a little more relaxed. "So does that mean you want to do him?" I continued.

"No, not do him, but it might be fun to play around with him a little." she admitted. "Are you serious about wanting to watch me or is that just part of the fantasy?"

I spoke quickly, "No, I think it would be really hot to see!"

"Are you serious?"

"You wouldn't be mad?"

"Wouldn't you be jealous?" I spoke as honestly as I could, "I wouldn't be mad unless you did it behind my back and yes, I would be jealous, but aroused too!"

"Well, he's just moved here from Chicago and doesn't know anyone here so, I could easily invite him to go out with us and see what happens."

"Are you really sure you want me to do it?"

She was smiling the sweetest little smile and I had a raging hardon, so how could I refuse?

On Thursday she came back from the club smiling from ear to ear. "I did it!"

"He said that he would be thrilled to go dancing with us Saturday night."

"He must have thanked me a dozen times before I left the gym."

"I told him that we would meet him at 9:00 at Jakes."

"Are you sure you want to do this?"

I assured her that it would be fun and exciting and that we could always back out if we didn't feel comfortable with it. I was a bundle of nerves for the next two days. What a funny feeling. I was very excited, nervous as hell, and a little jealous, but it certainly put a spark into our life! All I could think about was how hot Trish was. Over and over I pictured her flawless tits with their stiff dark upturned nipples, the way she tapers to a narrow waist before slightly flaring again to the most perfect little butt that you have ever seen.

She had already told me that there would be no intercourse, but that she would tease him and play a little in front of me. My pecker was stiff for two days. Trish is so fucking hot and he might get to see her goodies and . . . maybe, get to touch some! And I would get to watch her tease him. Watch her flaunt herself before him. Let him see what I have, let him want her . . . but know that she's mine!

Saturday finally arrived and I watched as Trish prepared to go out. She was obviously excited too, and took special care with her makeup and hair. As she buttoned her sundress I noticed that she wore only a white lace thong and her highest strappy heels. She really didn't need a bra because nothing showed and her breasts needed no support, but is was very sexy to know that she would be braless all night, with only those skimpy panties keeping her from being naked!

We arrived at the dance club first and were already seated at a table when Todd approached. Holy fucking shit! He was impeccably dressed in a dark blazer, white freshly starched button up shirt, and gray slacks. He was tall, and built like a line backer. Of course that didn't surprise me since I already knew he was a personal trainer . . . but he was black as coal! It's not that I had any objections or that it mattered to me, but Trish had grown up in a small town and as far as I knew had never known a black person in her life, so it came as quite a shock.

As we were introduced and began to get to know each other, I understood why Trish had been attracted. He was a hell of a guy, very relaxed and easy going, with a great sense of humor and polished manners. He quickly put us all at ease and repeatedly thanked us for our invitation.

As it turned out he was as accomplished a dancer as he was a conversationalist, and soon he and Trish were out on the dance floor. I was content with sipping my beer and watching them as they moved gracefully across the floor. Trish was having a great time and since I was no where near her league when it came to dancing, it was fun to watch her "cut a rug" so to speak. They danced almost every dance, breaking only when the band did, or to down some drink and visit a bit. I never tired of watching them and began to notice that as the night wore on and the drink began to take effect, they danced more suggestively.

Trish would shake her boobs at him as she thrashed her shoulders from side to side, turn and wiggle her ass against the front of his slacks. And she continually graced him with her dazzling smile. He seemed to hold her more closely, let his hands run down her side and back, or rest on her ass. I knew that he was be able to feel her naked tits flatten out against him and her bare ass cheeks beneath the thin fabric of her dress.

They began to draw a crowd to watch the sexy dance of the tiny young white girl and her black stud. And what a show they put on! She would literally straddle his leg and hunch his thigh as they moved to the music. During fast songs Trish would dance in close and moving to the rhythm of the beat, slowly move into a squat position until her face was even with, and only inches from, his fly. I am sure he was as hard as a rock . . . I know I was!

As one song set ended, Trish rose on her tip toes and Todd leaned down so they could kiss. I lost my breath, my heart skipped a beat, my stomach got queasy, and my dick began to throb! My beautiful, sweet, innocent wife had just kissed a black stranger with a raging hardon on a lighted stage before scores of straining eyes! And that kiss was obviously one of passion and promise!

Todd and Trish returned to the table and in hand. Todd couldn't have been more flattering. He told me how beautiful and charming my wife was and how lucky I was that she had chosen me to spend her life with. He said that he could only hope that some day he might find another woman as wonderful as mine to marry.

Then, Todd excused himself to the restroom . . . I think to give us a chance to talk privately. I hadn't seen Trish so excited in a long time. She was aroused, flustered, and almost breathless.

"Michael, are you sure you want to do this?"

"I would never do anything to cause a problem between you and me."

"We can call it a night right now if you want."

"We've had an exciting night, and can end it now."

I confided that I was hornier than I had been in quite a while and that her teasing was driving both Todd me wild. I asked her what she wanted to do. She surprised me again by saying that she had already told Todd that I wanted to watch her play sexually with another guy.

He said that he would love it, was pleased that we had chosen him and that, as I had guessed, he went to the restroom to give us time to decide. When Todd approached the table rather sheepishly, I stood, slapped him on the shoulder, and invited him to stop by the house for a night cap before he headed home. He broke into a huge smile and immediately agreed. Since I knew the "cat was out of the bag" and we lived so close to the club, I suggested that we all take our car and that I would take him back to his later.

The ride home took about fifteen minutes. Todd and Trish sat in the back and after a whole evening of teasing each other, it didn't take long before they moved together. I heard some rustling in the backseat and it became obvious that my wife had moved to sit on Todd's lap. They were directly behind me so I couldn't see, but Trish leaned forward to lay her forearms on the back of my seat so that her face was almost against my ear.

She began to whisper, "Oh my God, he's touching me . . . he's feeling my breasts. Her breath became short as she continued, "Oh, oh, you know what that does to me." A couple of pants later she cooed, "Michael, he unbuttoning my dress, and I'm going to let him." In a raspy voice I heard, "I can't believe we're doing this; he's playing with my bare tits and twisting my nipples!"

"He's pulling on them . . . oh!"

"Oh Michael!"

"Oh my God, Michael, I can feel his hard cock twitching underneath me."

My heart was pounding. I couldn't breathe or swallow. I couldn't see anything, but her panting play by play was even sexier! I drove faster, hoping that we could get home before too much more happened. And then she whimpered, "His hand is under my dress and moving up my thigh." followed by a sharp inhale and a soft, "Ahh . . . oh, oh." I knew that he had reached her lace panty, probably had it pushed to the side and maybe had a finger in my wife's sweet pussy.

How well I knew the touch of her tender distended lips and the moist core of the mouth of her sex . . . but it was his turn. My wife was sitting on a strangers lap, legs spread, allowing him to explore her wet aroused pussy! She had teased him all night, but finally he was getting his reward.

By the time we arrived at the apartment, Trish was already presentable and we walked on to our unit. I went to fix us a drink and get some prime smoke that I had put aside for a special occasion. When I returned to the living room I was pleased to see that although they had dimmed the lights, and were dancing to some soft music, they had not begun anything sexually while I was absent.

Todd and Trish joined me on the couch and we visited again while we enjoyed our drinks and smoke. I began to complement them on their graceful dance movements at the club, and teased them that they had captivated the attention of the whole room.

Todd took that as an invitation to ask Trish to dance again. This time, dancing just a couple of feet from me they danced more sensually to the soft romantic music. Todd held her close and dipped his head to brush his face against her hair and nuzzle at her neck, and she swayed in his arms with both arms around his neck and her cheek against his chest.

Todd slid his hand down the small of her back to come to rest on her firm ass. However this time he openly squeezed and fondled her ass as they danced while working the hem of her dress up inch by inch. She made no move to discourage him. I watched attentively as more thigh was revealed until the bottom of her globes peeked into the light and his fingers found bare skin.

He suddenly pushed the back of her skirt to her waist and claimed the only intimate part of her body he had not explored. She allowed him to run his hands freely across her naked skin, dipping his long black fingers into the crack between her cheeks.

To encourage his touch, she spread her legs slightly and rose to her tiptoes to allow his fingers to trace the satin string of the thong as it passed between her legs.

I watched my fantasy come to life before my eyes as he openly pet my wife's most private places. Their actions were incredibly arousing, but the contrast of their skin tones made their contact appear even more naughty and daring.

He released her dress to allow the hem to drop back to its normal position as he moved his hands to the sides of her head. Holding her petite head in his massive hands, he tilted her face up to kiss her sweetly on her lips, before moving his hands to trace the back of his fingers across her cheek, neck shoulder and the sides of her breasts. Oh my God, it was about to happen!

He was going to unbutton Trish's dress in front of me and she was going to let him. Trish back slightly to allow him space to unfasten her dress but continued to flutter sweet soft kisses on his lips and chin. She was definitely giving him the "green light" to continue.

Then it hit me like a tun of bricks. My darling beautiful wife had chosen to willingly give herself to her muscular buck. My mouth hung open and dry. I was barely breathing, and my stomach was doing flip flops. I could hardly sit still and wanted to scream for them to stop. My voice was caught in my throat when I began to see her through new eyes.

I had forgotten how alluring, how seductive, how sexy she could be! It was all new to him and he was obviously captivated by her seductive appeal and was excited that she was about to bless him with her feminine charms. Her gift to me was an opportunity to observe her intimate contact with fresh eyes. Suddenly my anxiety and fear was replaced with pride, lust and a sense of awe.

As that perspective sunk into my brain, her dress fluttered to the floor and she stood gloriously naked except for her panties and heels before an admiring stranger. My trance was broken as he spoke for the first time, "My God, you're a goddess!"

"I've never seen a more spectacular woman."

"You're even more beautiful than I imagined!" She stood patiently, arms at her sides, shoulders back and allowed her partner to enjoy her naked tits. Trish remained motionless as he traced the contours of her breasts with his fingertips before lifting them to test their weight and firmness.

He applied gentle pressure on her nipples, seeming enjoying the way they popped back into position, fully erect as his thumb passed over them proclaiming her arousal.

Trish smiled and melted back into his arms. I beamed with pride at his complementary observations. They continued to dance with him fully dressed and her almost naked in his embrace. In a few moments Trish unbuttoned his shirt and pushed is over his shoulders, baring his heavily muscled chest to her touch.

She sensuously stroked his pecks and fondled his abs until she reached and unfastened his belt buckle. Todd took her hint, stepped back a step, and dropped his shirt, shoes, socks and slacks to the floor. Now both in their underpants they stared at each other for a moment. Trish's eyes traveled down and back up his body before locking eyes with Todd.

With a flash in her eyes and a mischievous smile on her face, she pushed her panties to her ankles and displayed her naked, perfectly manicured pussy to his view. Following suite, he removed his boxers and allowed his manhood to bounce fully erect from his loin.

Then, each completely naked, they moved into each other's embrace. Trish reached forward to grasp the end of Todd's cock. With the underside of his ebony pole lying in the palm of her right hand and her fingers wrapped firmly around its girth, she pulled it slightly up and away from his body, cupping his balls in her left hand.

She didn't stroke him but held it in reverence as if she had picked up a precious but heavy trophy from a low shelf. She tilted her face back in invitation for him to kiss her. He bent at the neck as he caressed the side of her face with one hand and they began to trade soft, teasing, lingering kisses while his other hand tenderly explored the folds of her pussy.

They held that pose for what seemed minutes and I'll never forget it. She stood poised and still on tip toes in her heels, sharing tender "butterfly" kisses, cradling his black cock as if it were valuable Vencian glass, allowing him to play freely in the downy fur between her legs. With light circular caresses of her clit he soon had her audibly whimpering at his touch.

Before long she was hunching at his finger as it disappeared between her distended lips, stroking his dick and literally licking and sucking on his tongue as if it were a miniature cock!

I was overwhelmed with lust. Because to them I had faded into the woodwork as if I was no longer in the room, I was free to release my own cock and began to frantically beat my meat as I watched my wife perform in a live sex show just feet from my position! Oh my God . . . She was so beautiful and sexy!

It was like Trish was in another world, parting her legs, and wildly hunching his fingers; releasing his tongue from her lips only long enough to babble incoherently, moan and whimper. He whispered something to her and then pushed on her shoulders to direct her to her knees.

104

In her kneeling position his swollen ebony cock hung just inches over her upturned face. There was an undeniable submission in her eyes that I had never seen as she stared at his meat. He gave her a long look and then to my surprise turned abruptly and stepped to the couch with his cock bobbing before him.

He sat on the edge of the couch next to me and lay back against the cushions with his legs widely parted. What happened next just blew my mind. He locked eyes with her and ordered, "Come here!" I had never seen anything like it.

Never losing eye contact she began to crawl, breasts hanging, the muscles on her ass and flanks rippling like a cheetah stalking her prey. Upon reaching her goal she used the flat of her tongue to lick, ever so slowly, across his dangling black ball sack, up the length of his shaft to kiss him tenderly on the tip.

"Oh yeah," he moaned, "lick my nuts."

I was worrying about how far she was going to let things go, but also so aroused that I could not speak. I sat there stroking my cock and stared as she dipped down deeper between his legs and began to paint his scrotum with soft strokes of her tongue.

"That's it, baby . . . lick them all over . . . lick them good!"

"You like licking my balls, don't you baby?"

"I know you like it."

When his balls were shiny with her saliva, she again licked back to the crown. This time he pushed against the back of her head in encouragement and directed,

"Suck it down, baby."

"Suck it all the way down!"

I watched in amazement as his cock disappeared down her throat. Pangs of jealousy wracked my mind as he inserted his black dick to the hilt. With her lips stretched to accommodate the girth of its base, he instructed, "Look at me, Trish." With her mouth stuffed with cock and his balls pressed against her chin she flashed open those pleading baby blues.

I had never seen anything so sexy and so decadent in my life. In one more test of trust, he reached forward and squeezed her nostrils shut. Her eyes grew wider but she waited breathlessly, her mouth and throat stuffed with cock, her eyes tearing.

After what seemed like an eternity, he released both her nose and the back of her head. She popped off is cock, gagging and gasping for air. Tears were running down her angelic face, her mouth gaped open to show ribbons of saliva and precum clinging from the roof of her mouth and tongue. I thought she would be pissed and started to go to her rescue, when she gasped, "Give it to me!"

www.ingramcontent.com/pod-product-compliance
Lightning Source LLC
Chambersburg PA
CBHW050310260626
47156CB00005B/1735